FIFE COUNCIL LIBRARIES

FC412872

KT-452-567

*a*t.

J

A Bullet for the Preacher

When a preacher is shot dead in the quiet town of Bircher, his brother, Roland Payne, arrives with the intention of avenging his death. He accepts the post of deputy sheriff in the hope of finding the killer and, along the way, he unearths a feud between an old-established family, the Lamptons, and some newcomers to the town, the Olsens, one of whom is the beautiful Hedda Olsen.

Roland's life is threatened as he is caught between the two families, but which one should he support? Eventually he discovers the identity of his brother's murderer but when the final shoot-out arrives the death toll is high and Roland's future is in the balance.

A Bullet for the Preacher

Ron Watkins

A Black Horse Western

ROBERT HALE · LONDON

© Ron Watkins 2003
First published in Great Britain 2003

ISBN 0 7090 7367 4

Robert Hale Limited
Clerkenwell House
Clerkenwell Green
London EC1R 0HT

The right of Ron Watkins to be identified as
author of this work has been asserted by him
in accordance with the Copyright, Designs and
Patents Act 1988.

FIFE COUNCIL LIBRARIES	
FC412872	
CAW	16/10/2003
F	£10.75
	BR

Typeset by
Derek Doyle & Associates, Liverpool.
Printed and bound in Great Britain by
Antony Rowe Limited, Wiltshire

CHAPTER 1

When John Payne arrived in the town of Bircher his first reaction was to move on. The stage had stopped there for an hour – long enough for passengers to have a meal and stretch their legs before the stage headed further west.

John's first reaction was strengthened after walking along the length of Main Street. It comprised the usual collection of a livery stable, several saloons, a couple of banks, a sadler's and a blacksmith's shop. In addition there were a couple of tea rooms, a run-down hotel, a gun shop, a couple of clothes shops and an apothecary's. John stopped outside the apothecary's.

It was a dingy shop which advertized cures for a variety of ills on cards in the window. One of the cards advertized a universal cure for illnesses from rheumatism to croup, named Gregory's balsam. There were other cards advertizing instant cures for whooping-cough, scabies, chickenpox, influenza and ingrowing toenails. However the card that held John's attention stated: 'Preacher wanted. Apply Town Clerk'.

John hesitated. He stared at the notice again. Bircher didn't look the kind of small town that had a church. Suddenly he came to a decision. He had nothing to lose by finding out about the situation. He opened the door.

A bell attached to the door announced his entrance. A small middle-aged man appeared from a back room.

'What can I get you?' he demanded.

'Actually, I don't need anything. Just some information. I'm enquiring about the card in the window that says, "Preacher Wanted".'

'Are you a preacher?' The small man peered up at John as though half-expecting to see some evidence of his profession about his person, such as him carrying a Bible.

'I was a preacher. In Boston.'

'Boston? That's a long way away.'

'Most people who end up here come from a long way away,' said John, patiently.

'Yes, I suppose so,' said the other, scratching his chin, thoughtfully.

'Well, where do I find the town clerk?' demanded John.

'Your best bet is to call in the sheriff's office. The town clerk is the sheriff's brother.'

'Where will I find the sheriff's office?'

'About fifty yards further along the street.'

John came out of the shop into the warm afternoon air. He had a choice. Either carry on further along the street until he came to the sheriff's office, or turn back. The stage wouldn't be going for half an hour. He still had time to grab a bite to eat in one of the tea rooms. After all, not only did Bircher have little to recommend it, but it also seemed to suffer from a bad case of nepotism – with the two top jobs sewn up. The sheriff running the one and his brother the other.

On impulse he stepped inside the tea room. There were only four tables in the shop. They were all occupied by women of assorted ages. John was on the point of turning and leaving when one of the younger women indicated a free chair by her table.

'There's room here,' she said, with a winning smile.

'Thanks,' said John, taking the proffered seat.

A middle-aged woman came over to take his order. John hesitated.

'I can recommend the apple-pie,' said the young woman opposite.

'Thanks,' said John. 'I'll try it.'

When the pie arrived he was glad he had followed the advice. It was fresh and tasty. His companion smiled to see how he was evidently enjoying it.

'I haven't eaten all day,' he explained, when he

had cleared the last morsel of pastry from his plate. 'I've just come in on the stage.'

'And you'll be leaving shortly,' she retorted.

He couldn't help noticing the bitterness in her voice. He had already noticed her attractive face with startling blue eyes and fair curls rising above a wide forehead.

'Well – yes, I suppose so.' Why did he sound almost apologetic? After all they were complete strangers.

Well, at the next moment not quite complete. 'I'm May Stanfield,' she said, offering her hand.

'I'm John Payne.'

Was it his imagination, or did they hold hands for a fraction of a second longer that it was customary? Don't let yourself get carried away by a pretty face. It was to get away from one such face that you travelled west, he reminded himself.

There was an awkward silence. He glanced surreptitiously at the clock on the wall. It was still minutes before the stage left. He would make his excuses now.

However her next words stopped him.

'Are you a gunslinger?'

'No, I'm not,' he replied, indignantly. 'I'm a preacher.'

'A preacher?' There was excitement in her voice.

'Yes. I used to preach in Boston.'

Why was she staring at him so intently with

those beautiful eyes?

'Then you could be the answer to our prayers. Except of course that you're moving on,' she concluded, bitterly.

'Yes, I really must be going now. Or I'll miss the stage.' He stood up.

She was staring at the table. She didn't even acknowledge his move. He stared at her bowed head. She really was pretty. Even with her mouth set in a determined sullen line, she was still pretty.

He moved towards the door. He was still half-expecting her to look up. But she didn't do so. He left the tea room with disappointment being his uppermost feeling.

He arrived at the stage. He realized that he was the last to arrive. All the other passengers were in their seats. They stared at him with hardly concealed hostility for keeping them waiting, although it was barely two minutes past two o'clock.

He was about to step up on the stage when he made a momentous decision.

'I'm not coming,' he informed the driver.

The driver shrugged his shoulders. It was nothing to him whether a passenger changed his mind.

Back in the tea room May was still seated at the table. She was idly toying with a tea spoon. When she saw John her face lit up.

'You're staying?' she exclaimed delightedly.

CHAPTER 2

John had no difficulty in finding the sheriff's office. It was a low, squat, stone building. The front door was open. He knocked and went in.

The sheriff was seated behind a desk. He was a thickset man with a red, bloated face. He had watchful eyes and was chewing tobacco.

'What can I do for you, mister?' he demanded.

'I've come about the card in the apothecary's window. The one saying you need a preacher.'

The sheriff took his time before replying. He moved the tobacco round a few times in his mouth. Finally he spat into the spittoon which was by the side of his desk.

'What's your name, mister?' he demanded.

'John Payne.'

'You're not from these parts?'

'No. I'm from Boston.'

'It's a long way from Boston to Bircher,' said the sheriff, eyeing John, thoughtfully.

'I thought I could serve God more usefully in the West than in Boston,' said John, drily.

'You'd better sit down,' said the sheriff. He indicated the only spare chair in the office.

'Where will I find the town clerk?' asked John.

'I'm afraid you won't find him. At least, not at the moment. He's out of town.'

'So what happens about my application for the preacher's post? Who do I see now?'

'Me,' replied the sheriff, leaning back in his chair and tucking his thumbs under the lapels of his jacket.

John was taken aback. 'Right,' he said, pulling himself together. 'If you'll tell me whether I've got the job or not, maybe we can go from there.'

'Oh, you've got the job,' stated the sheriff positively. 'You can start right away.'

'How much will I be paid?'

'Twenty dollars a week. Will that suit you?'

John had to admit that that was more than he had expected. In a small town like this he would have settled for less.

'Yes, that's all right,' he confirmed.

'You want to find some lodgings,' suggested the sheriff. 'Mrs Pine is where the last preacher was staying. She's a widow.'

He gave John directions how to find her cottage. John stood up. He half-expected the sheriff to stand to see him out. Instead the sheriff cut himself another piece of tobacco.

'Don't shut the door,' he called after him.

This is the West, not Boston, John reminded himself as he walked towards Mrs Pine's cottage. You wouldn't expect to find the refinements of behaviour here that you would find in Boston.

Mrs Pine's home was a neat white cottage with honeysuckle growing round the porch. John knocked. A small elderly woman wearing an apron came to the door.

John introduced himself. She peered up at him as though trying to confirm whether he would be a suitable lodger. He must have passed the test because, after a few moments, she said, 'You'd better come in.'

She led the way into a small sitting-room. A fluffy white cat which was sitting on the mat regarded him suspiciously.

'This is Mr Payne, Snowy.' Mrs Pine introduced him to the cat. 'He's going to have Mr Manford's room.'

'He was your last lodger?' enquired John, tickling the cat behind the ear.

'Yes, he was with us for a few months before he passed on.'

Snowy obviously approved of being tickled behind the ear. He rolled on to his back.

'He was the previous preacher of the town?'

'That's right. He was about your age. He was a nice young man.'

Snowy decided that he would get better treatment if he was closer to John. He jumped up on the sofa beside him.

'What did he die of?'

'Didn't the sheriff tell you? He was shot.'

CHAPTER 3

After a tasty meal of beef-stew John asked Mrs Pine where he would find the church. She gave him instructions.

'It's on Moss Lampton's land. It's about half a mile outside the town. You can't miss it.'

John set out. It was a fine evening. The sort of evening where you thanked God that you were alive and could enjoy it. The only cloud on the horizon was the fact that his predecessor, Manford, had been shot. He went over the sparse details Mrs Pine had supplied.

She said that he had gone to the church on Sunday morning. It was to have been a special service – a christening. The baby to be christened was Moss Lampton's grandson. Only the immediate family had been invited. These consisted of Moss Lampton, his son Nicholas, the daughter-in-law Helen, and members of another family, the Powers. Apparently Manford had been half-way

15

through the christening service when the tragedy occurred. There was the sound of a shot. The church window was shattered. To the horrified onlookers the preacher collapsed in a pool of blood. It was obvious that he was dead.

The men rushed outside the church to try to spot the gunman. He had obviously used a rifle and therefore he could be some distance away. The men spread out and tried to search the terrain around the church. It was rough, stony land which was the main reason the church had been built on that particular spot in the first place, since the land couldn't be used for grazing cattle. It was therefore easy for the gunman to slip away without being spotted.

John had asked Mrs Pine what the sheriff had made of the shooting.

'Him!' Mrs Pine replied, scornfully. 'He couldn't spot a killer if he carried a billboard with "killer" printed on it.'

John arrived at the church. It was a stone building with a tin roof. John glanced at the roof with misgiving. He reckoned that if it rained during his service the congregation wouldn't stand much chance of hearing it. On the other hand maybe some of the congregation would consider it a fortunate reprieve. He smiled at the thought.

He opened the door with the key Mrs Pine had given him. The inside had the familiar musty smell. There were neat piles of hymn books on

16

the front bench ready to be handed out to the congregation. John picked up the top one. It was the standard hymn book. It had been well used judging by its condition. However he liked to see worn hymn books. It reflected on their regular use. It meant that the church was an essential part of the community with a regular number in the congregation. He counted the hymn books. Forty. That wasn't bad for a town this size. He would be reasonably happy with a congregation of forty to start with. After that it would be up to him to try to increase it.

He stepped up to the pulpit. The Bible was in its place. It was a handsome Bible with gold lettering on the cover and a gold border. He opened it. Inside the cover he read: 'This Bible has been donated to the people of Bircher by Mr Moss Lampton'.

So Moss Lampton had supplied not only the land where the church stood but also the Bible. He certainly seemed to be a generous person. Maybe his next step should be to pay Mr Lampton a visit.

He went through the church door after first kneeling down to utter a short prayer. He locked the door after him. The problem was, which way was the Lampton ranch? He spotted a man in the adjoining churchyard. He was an elderly man with white hair and thin moustache.

'Excuse me, could you tell me how to get to the

Lampton ranch?' asked John.

The man regarded him steadily. 'You'd be the new preacher?' he demanded.

'That's right. My name is John Payne.'

'I'm Charles Brewer. I help to keep the church tidy. And the churchyard.'

'Pleased to meet you.' They shook hands.

'The Lampton ranch? It's about a mile down this lane. This is the quickest way to get there.'

John thanked him. 'I expect I'll see you at the service on Sunday,' he added.

'Oh, I'll be there,' replied Mr Brewer. 'I wouldn't miss it for the world.'

What did Brewer mean by that? John wondered as he set off down the lane.

He found the Lampton ranch without any difficulty. It was a long, low, wooden building. There was a veranda in the front and some cowboys had gathered there. From their laughter it was obvious they were playing some game or other.

As John drew nearer he could see what it was. The cowboys were firing at a target and, judging from their hilarity the person with the pistol wasn't having much success with his shooting. There were about half a dozen cowboys engaged in the game and although they appeared engrossed in it, John realized that at least a couple of them were watching him closely as he approached.

'Is Moss Lampton in?' he enquired of the nearest cowboy.

They had stopped their game and now he was the object of their collective stares.

'He's gone to market,' replied the cowboy. 'He won't be back for a couple of days.'

Having delivered this information he was about to return to their game when a thought obviously struck him.

'Hey, mister! You wouldn't want to join in?'

'Ten cents a try,' announced another. 'You've got to try to hit the coin that Charlie spins into the air.'

'If you hit it you collect all that's in the hat.' He tipped the hat he was holding to show John that it contained a score or so of ten-cent pieces.

John's first reaction was to refuse. Then on impulse he changed his mind. 'All right, I'll give it a try,' he stated.

Some of the cowboys grinned openly. If the greenhorn thought that he was going to hit Charlie's spinning silver dollar he was going to be mightily mistaken.

'You have to draw as well as shoot,' explained one of the cowboys.

They fixed a belt round John's waist. He pulled the gun experimentally out of its holster and slid it back in. He pushed the belt a couple of inches further down his waist. He seemed in no hurry to begin his shot. The grins were still on the faces of most of the cowboys. The exception was the cowboy who had asked him to join in the game in the first place. His name was Mallard. He watched, fascinated, as John moved the belt another fraction until he was satisfied that it was in the right position.

Finally John nodded to show that he was ready. Charlie licked his lips in anticipation. He was standing about twenty yards from the stranger. He knew that when he spun that silver dollar high in the air there was no way that he would draw in time to hit it before it fell to the ground.

'I'm ready,' said John.

Charlie spun the coin. A blur of movement from John and the *crack* of the revolver seemed to come at the same time.

There was no doubt about it. He had hit it. The cowboys gathered round the silver dollar which lay on the ground like a squashed flower. No one ventured to pick it up.

The reactions when they came were mixed.

'That was great shooting,' said one.

'That's the first time that anyone has done it for ages,' said another.

'I bet you can't do it again,' said another.

John glanced around at their faces. It was obvious that the last speaker had sown the seeds of doubt in their minds.

'It was luck,' said another.

John sighed. He produced a silver dollar of his own. 'You can use mine this time,' he stated, tossing it to Charlie.

Charlie had secretly decided to make this shot even more difficult. While the stranger was sheathing his revolver he surreptitiously moved a few yards further away. He was now about twenty-five yards from John.

John glanced at him to gauge the new distance. The cowboys had been aware of Charlie's move. The smiles slowly came back to their faces as they realized the difficulty the distance now presented.

'Right!' snapped John.

The coin spun high into the air, the sun's rays catching it in flight. Suddenly there was the *crack* of the shot and the dollar dropped to the ground.

'He's done it again,' said one of the cowboys, unnecessarily.

This time one of them picked up the coin. He handed it back to John, almost reverently.

'Are you a gunslinger?' asked Mallard.

They waited with eager anticipation for his reply.

'No, I'm not,' replied John.

'Well, you've won all this.' One of the cowboys offered him the hat containing the ten-cent pieces.

'I'm the new preacher,' announced John. 'I'll make a bargain with you. If you all agree to come to church on Sunday you can keep the money and carry on with your game.'

John only just managed to keep a straight face at their expressions of surprise.

CHAPTER 4

On Sunday the church was packed. It was not only packed but there were people who had not been able to get in. These were seated happily on the ground outside the church. It was a fine evening and some of the men preferred their choice of seat since it meant that they could listen to the service and enjoy a smoke at the same time.

John had obligingly left the church door open. His voice was loud enough to be heard outside. He started with a short prayer. Then he announced that they would sing the hymn, 'Rock of Ages'. This was a perennial favourite and the congregation outside, which numbered almost as many as inside joined in with gusto.

John's service was based on the commandment: 'Thou shall not kill'. He explained how the West was becoming more and more lawless. However killing wasn't the answer to the problem. People when confronted with a situation where killing could be one solution, should choose the Biblical answer, and walk away. The last hymn was another one where the congregation outside knew the words and could therefore join in. It was, 'We'll All Gather at the River.'

As the familiar words echoed round the church, John glanced around. Judging by the number in the congregation his first service seemed to have been a success. He couldn't help, though, glancing at the window which had been shattered when his predecessor had been killed. He could see the low hill behind where the gunman must have been hiding. He hastily turned his attention to the singing. 'We'll all gather at the river, the beautiful, the beautiful river.'

He glanced around at the congregation. Why did his gaze keep on coming back to May Stanfield? She was pretty, yes. In fact he had taken in most of the women's faces in the congregation from his vantage point in the pulpit and there was no doubt that she was the prettiest there. She knew he had glanced at her from time to time and had given him a warm smile. What had Mrs Pine said about her? Her husband had died about a year back having contracted influenza which had developed into double pneumonia. So he had died after a short illness. He had left May fairly well provided for since he had been the town lawyer and had been responsible for many of the deeds relating to the transfers of properties a few years back. She had added, 'You could do worse than marrying the pretty widow.'

His reply had been, 'I'm sorry, but I'm not the marrying kind.'

Mrs Pine had given him a quizzical look but had refrained from pressing the point.

John closed with a short prayer and the service was over.

'That's the kind of service I like,' said Mallard. 'Short and to the point.'

'He doesn't expect us to come here every Sunday, does he?' asked one of Lampton's cowboys.

'I think he only said today,' ventured another. They glanced at Mallard for confirmation. He was generally regarded among the cowboys as the one with the brains.

'The agreement was for today only,' confirmed Mallard. 'Although if he keeps his services as short as that, I'll probably come next week.'

'Well I won't be coming,' said Charlie. 'We're wasting valuable poker time by coming here.'

There was a chorus of assent from the others.

Although Lampton's cowboys were happy with the brevity of the service, some of the church dignitaries were less than pleased. In fact when John was shaking hands with them as they left the church, one of them voiced his concern.

He was a tall, thin man who was accompanied

by a very small woman.

'Excuse me, preacher,' he stated, when it came to his turn to shake John's hand. 'My name is Purdy. I'd just like to say that I enjoyed the service. What there was of it.'

'You think it was rather short?' queried John.

'Of course it's not my place to question the length of your service, but your predecessor did have longer services. He was very popular.'

'The preacher who was shot, Mr Manford?'

Mr Purdy stared at John suspiciously. Was he being supercilious? He judged from the innocent expression on John's face that he wasn't.

'Well perhaps you'll think about it,' was his parting shot.

The moment came which John was anticipating with mixed feelings. May Stanfield came up to him to shake his hand.

'That was a lovely service,' she said.

'I've just been criticized for keeping it too short,' John informed her.

'Who by? No, let me guess. Mr Purdy.'

'The same.'

'Well don't take any notice of him. If it had been longer he'd have criticized you for making it too long.'

John smiled. She really was a tonic. However his smile slipped when she ventured her next question.

'Would you like to come to my house for tea,

one day? My housekeeper makes a selection of cakes which I think could tempt you.'

He hesitated for a split second. He knew what the reply had to be although he would have given anything not to have to say it.

'I'm sorry. I'll be busy for the next few weeks. I don't think I'll be able to find the time.'

She couldn't conceal the sudden hurt on her face.

'Some other time perhaps.' She uttered the words in confusion, before turning on her heel.

CHAPTER 5

The following day Moss Lampton was due to return from market. John waited until the afternoon before calling at his ranch.

This time there was no sign of the cowboys who were obviously out on the range. John was ushered into the living-room by an elderly housekeeper. There he found two men each with a glass of whiskey in front of them.

The elder of the two stood up. 'I'm Moss Lampton,' he announced, as he shook hands with John. 'And this is my nephew Len Childs.'

John shook hands with Childs. He was stocky in build like his uncle, but was about a head shorter. The main difference to John, however, was that while Moss had a pleasant, round face with even features, Childs had a thin mouth and wary eyes which made you distrust him on first sight. John hoped that his first impression would prove erroneous.

'Len has come back with me from Crichton. He'll be staying with me for a while.'

'Permanently, I hope, uncle,' replied Childs, with a sly smile.

'When I was at the market I bought a Hereford bull,' continued Moss. 'He's a beauty.'

John smiled at Moss's obvious enthusiasm.

'Do you know anything about bulls, Mr Payne? No, I'm sorry, I forgot. You're a preacher. Anyhow, where are my manners? Can I offer you a drink?'

'I don't drink,' John replied.

Moss couldn't keep the surprise out of his voice. 'Your predecessor often took a glass of whiskey with me.'

'Even Jesus drank wine,' announced Childs.

'I know. Everybody has their own choice,' stated John.

Moss accepted the decision. He asked what other drink John would have. He chose coffee. When the housekeeper was making it Moss turned to John.

'I hear you're an expert with a revolver.'

Childs, who had picked up a magazine, looked up with surprise.

'I managed to beat your cowboys,' stated John. 'I don't think any of them are experts with a gun.'

'So you're fast,' said Childs, thoughtfully.

'Sign of a misspent youth,' said John, lightly.

He was relieved of any further explanations by

the arrival of his coffee.

'I hear your first service was quite a success,' said Moss. 'There was a crowd outside the church as well as inside.'

'I expect a great deal of it was due to curiosity,' said John. 'The real test will come next Sunday.' He added, 'One of the main reasons I've come here is to thank you for donating the church.'

'I was in a financial position to do it. So I did it.'

'It was very generous of you. I'm sure the people of Bircher appreciate it.'

'I expect most of them do,' Moss agreed. 'Although there are one or two who would like to see me buried in the churchyard.'

John guessed that Moss was referring to his neighbouring rancher, Nils Olsen. Mrs Pine had given him some details about the feud between the two men, but John wanted to hear it from Moss himself.

'How did it all start?' he asked.

'It started two years ago when Olsen came to Bircher,' said Moss, bitterly. 'He bought the ranch next to mine. It was run down – old Sam Peters had spent most of his time drinking instead of looking after the ranch. Anyhow Nils bought it. I assumed he was going to raise cattle the same way as Sam had. Instead, do you know what he did?'

John already knew from his prime source of information, Mrs Pine, but he feigned ignorance. 'No.'

'He planted corn. Would you believe it? This is cattle country. It has always been cattle country. My grandfather came here and fought the Indians to establish this ranch. He was killed here. My father and mother died here. My wife died here – and they are all buried on the range – there was no church then.' His voice had risen.

'Take it easy, Uncle,' advised Childs.

'How can I take it easy when that bastard has fenced off the range and denied my cattle access to water which they've been entitled to since my grandfather arrived here.'

He stood up and thumped the table to emphasize his point. John's cup jumped a couple of inches in surprise.

'We'll sort something out, Uncle,' said Childs, placatingly, putting his hand over his uncle's.

What exactly did he mean by that, wondered John, as ten minutes later he walked slowly back to the town.

CHAPTER 6

John knew that his next duty was to call on Nils Olsen. Mrs Pine had warned him against calling there.

'They're not like us,' she had stated. 'They keep themselves to themselves. They've never mixed with the community.'

'It's my duty to call to see them,' John had replied stubbornly.

There were acres and acres of golden corn. He ran his hand through the heads as he walked along. He picked one of them and rubbed it between his hands. The movements released the ears of corn. He put one in his mouth and began to chew it. As he walked he could see the ranch in the distance about half a mile away. There was no sign of the usual cowboys that he associated with a ranch. In fact the first inkling that there was another human being within distance was when he heard the sound of the *crack* of a rifle and a bullet whistled past his ear.

John dived into the corn. Shock and fear struggled to gain supremacy among his conflicting emotions. Fear gained the uppermost hand. Why had the unknown gunman shot at him? Perhaps he had been mistaken for somebody else. Nobody could have shot at him on purpose since he had no enemies in Bircher. He had only arrived a couple of days ago. Now he was already beginning to wish he hadn't come at all. Particularly when a second bullet churned through the corn above his head.

One thing was sure. It wouldn't be safe for him to put his head above the level of the top of the corn. So that meant him crawling through the corn. It was something he didn't have to think twice about. He began to crawl back the way he had come.

He had gone about fifty yards at an uncomfortably slow pace when a couple of shots in quick succession reminded him that the rifleman was still searching for him. Not only that but he had a fair idea where he was since the bullets were uncomfortably close.

His main emotion of fear was suddenly replaced by anger. What right had the unknown gunman to be shooting at him? He was an innocent traveller. The bastard could have seriously injured him. Or even killed him.

The seething anger spurred an idea. It was no

good him crawling at a snail's pace back to the gate. The gunman would catch up with him long before he reached it. He would spot him down among the corn. Then the next rifle-shots would be more accurate. And it would be the angelic hosts and the pearly gates for him.

Well, whatever happened he wasn't going to die like a dog among the corn. There was only one alternative. It would require calling on bravery which he didn't know whether he had. Another searching bullet reminded him that now was the time to find out.

John shot up. He started to sprint towards the gate. As he went he zigzagged to try to put the gunman off his aim. For a few moments he thought his ruse had worked. He was within a hundred yards of the gate. It beckoned like a friendly haven. Moss Lampton's ranch and safety lay on the other side. John had almost started counting his blessings when there was the sound of another shot. This one was uncomfortably close. In fact he wondered whether it had nicked his ear.

He didn't stop to find out. He zigzagged once more even though it meant him losing a split second in his effort to reach the gate. There was the sound of another shot. John knew at once that this one had found its target. There was a stinging pain at the side of his head. He involuntarily put his hand to it. He felt something sticky which he knew instinctively was blood.

He had no time to investigate further. The gate was now only a few yards away. Spurred on by the blood in his hair he dived for it. He jumped over. He was about to land on the safety of the other side when a bullet hit him in the back. As he fell he realized that this time it wasn't merely a flesh wound.

CHAPTER 7

Folks say that John Payne's funeral was the biggest ever to be held in Bircher. All the local people attended and they even came from as far afield as Crichton. In fact it was from Crichton that the preacher came to hold the memorial service. He was an elderly man with white whiskers who was a firm believer in eternal damnation.

'The man who shot our brother, John,' he roared, 'will surely burn in hell.' There were shouts of 'Hallelujah' from the congregation.

'Whoever he is, and wherever he is,' continued the Reverend Landis, 'he will surely be confined to burn for eternity. There will be no escape for him. To gun down an innocent man is one of the worst crimes a human being can commit. But to gun down a servant of the Lord means there is no retribution. His punishment will be worse than the punishment of Doctor Faustus who sold his soul to the devil. Faustus found too late that there was no turning back. The wretched man who shot our brother, John, will also find that there is no hope for him. He will be committed to eternal damnation.'

In the short time that John had been in Bircher he had made a big impression on the community even though he had only held one service. The person who missed him most was the one who was in contact with him every day, Mrs Pine. A few of her friends returned to her house after the service. She had made tea and was handing cakes around.

'He was a lovely man,' she eulogized. 'He was so polite. He always said "please" and "thank you". Not like the riff-raff who're coming into Bircher these days.'

'Are they any nearer finding out who shot him?' asked one of the ladies.

'Huh,' said Mrs Pine, scornfully. 'The sheriff couldn't even find out who killed Mr Manford. I'd stand more chance of finding the killer myself.'

'They say that the sheriff is getting a posse together to go to the Olsen ranch,' ventured another. 'But that he was persuaded to leave it until after the funeral. Out of respect for Mr Payne.'

'I told him not to go,' said Mrs Pine, with sudden emotion. 'If he had listened to me he would be alive today.'

Another woman who was sharing her feeling was May Stanfield. In fact her eyes were red with crying.

'I've never cried so much since my husband died,' she told her best friend, Ivy.

'We'll all miss him,' agreed Ivy.

'You don't understand,' said May, vehemently. 'If it hadn't been for me he'd still be alive. I advised him to stay in Bircher.'

'Yes, but surely it was his own decision,' stated Ivy.

'He was on his way further west. The stage stopped here for an hour. He came into Laurie's café. I was in the café at the time.'

'I didn't know that,' said Ivy, interestedly.

'I'm sure if I hadn't persuaded him to stay, he'd have caught the stage and gone on west,' said May, dejectedly.

'You don't know that for sure,' objected Ivy. 'You don't know whether it's true.'

'I saw the way he looked at me during his service. Even though he said afterwards he couldn't come back for tea.'

'You mean there might have been a budding romance between you and Mr Payne?' asked a stunned Ivy.

'No, I don't,' said May, angrily. 'All I meant was that we could have been good friends.'

'All right, there's no need to snap my head off,' protested Ivy.

CHAPTER 8

The sheriff gathered together a posse of twelve men although he could have easily had twice that number. He refused to accept any men from Moss Lampton's ranch although he was told all the cowboys had volunteered, particularly those who had been beaten by John in the friendly shoot-out.

They gathered outside the sheriff's office at eleven o'clock. They were all eager to get to the Olsen ranch, although they had to listen to the sheriff's speech first.

'I don't want any shooting until I give the order,' he said. 'It's obvious that somebody from the Olsen ranch shot the preacher and probably shot the other preacher as well. When we get to the ranch I'll go inside. You'll all stay outside. If I think that one of the Olsens shot the preacher then I'll bring him out. I still don't want any of you to shoot him. We've got to do things properly.

We'll bring him back here. Then we'll hang the bastard.'

They were loud shouts of 'Hurrah!' and some of the men threw their hats into the air.

They set off in single file with the sheriff leading. When they came to the gate leading to the cornfields the sheriff opened it. The riders filed through, the last one not bothering to shut the gate.

They made their way to the ranch in the distance, deliberately trampling down the corn as they went. There was no one in sight. Some of the riders had drawn their guns, remembering how the preacher had been ambushed. They were within a couple of hundred yards of the ranch when suddenly three men with rifles appeared. They were standing behind a stone wall which effectively gave them excellent cover from the posse.

'It's old man Olsen and his two sons,' stated one of the riders.

Olsen was a large man. Even though in his fifties it was obvious that he still had a strong physique.

'That's far enough,' he said.

The posse reined in their horses.

'This is a legal posse,' shouted the sheriff. 'All the men have been sworn in. Somebody from your ranch killed the preacher. If you give him up we'll take him back with us.'

'There are only three people in my house who

can use guns,' said Mr Olsen. 'My sons and myself. I didn't shoot your preacher. Neither did my sons, Sven and Nils.' He waved a hand to indicate his two sons. One, a younger version of himself, looked as strong as his father would have been in his younger days; the other was thinner and looked more an academic than a farmer.

'That's what you say,' retorted the sheriff. 'But somebody from your ranch shot him. There are witnesses from Moss Lampton's ranch who saw him fall when he reached the gate. He had been coming to visit you. He was shot by somebody in your field.'

'I'm sorry about the preacher,' stated Mr Olsen. 'But I swear that none of us three killed him.'

'Who else is in your house?' demanded the sheriff.

'My wife Nora and my daughter Hedda.'

'What about the men working for you?'

'I haven't got any. We do all the work ourselves. Except when we need workmen to help us to cut the corn.'

'Let's take them all in,' suggested one of the posse. 'One of them will confess when they're all in jail.'

'You won't take us,' shouted Mr Olsen. 'We'll die first.'

'Take it easy, Pa,' said Nils. 'The sheriff's only doing his duty.'

'That's right,' asserted the sheriff. 'And my duty is to take you in for questioning.'

'I'm telling you none of us killed the preacher,' stated Mr Olsen, emphatically.

They had obviously reached an impasse. Some of the posse were muttering among themselves. What had started off as a promising adventure with the possibility of a hanging at the end had turned sour. A few of them had already wheeled their horses so that they were facing the direction from which they had come.

The sheriff realized the futility of any further confrontation. He reluctantly played his last card.

'I'll be getting in touch with the county marshal. If you don't co-operate you will have your land seized by the authorities.'

'Don't listen to him, Pa. He's bluffing,' said Nils.

The sheriff was determined to have the last word.

'Don't think you've heard the last of this,' he snapped, as he turned his horse round.

CHAPTER 9

It was about a fortnight later when Mrs Pine thought that she had seen a ghost. She had finished her dusting and cleaning in the morning – she had always contended that cleanliness was next to godliness – and afterwards she had dressed ready to go out shopping. In fact she was about to put on her hat. It was a well-worn brown felt hat which had seen many years' service, but she believed in thrift being an essential quality in one's life and she reckoned that the old hat still had a few years left to run.

As she related the story many times over, she was about to put the hatpin in her hat when there was a knock at the door. It's strange how in some moments of your life you're able to remember exactly what you were doing when something dramatic happened. It was a knock she didn't recognize. She knew her regular visitors – the half-dozen or so friends who would drop in from time to time for a gossip and a cup of tea. She instantly recognized that this wasn't one of them. It was a louder knock. The sort of knock of a person who had some urgent business with her.

Her next thought was that it could be one of her neighbours who was in trouble. From time to time she would be called upon to look after a small child while the mother went for the doctor because another member of the family was ill. Or maybe a neighbour would wish to borrow something urgently. She was regarded as a good neighbour in this respect and would help anybody if she could possibly do so. After all, wasn't it one of the principles of the gospel to help thy neighbour?

The knock came again.

'All right, hold your horses,' said Mrs Pine.

She opened the door. It was then she saw the ghost.

As she related afterwards, 'I don't know how I didn't faint. There he was, standing there as large as life.'

In answer to the audience's question, 'Who?' she would answer, 'Why, John Payne, of course.'

Each time she related the story the silence that greeted the revelation would be almost as huge as the silence that lasted when she saw the man standing there.

'Ye-es,' she finally gasped.

'You are Mrs Pine?'

She was aware that she had gone pale. 'Yes.'

'You sent me some of John's things.'

Relief flooded through her veins. 'You're related to John.'

'That's right. I'm his brother. His twin brother.'

'You're. . . ?'

'Roland. We were identical twins.'

Ten minutes later, a fully recovered Mrs Pine was pouring him a cup of tea in the kitchen.

'It's like seeing a ghost,' she couldn't help observing.

'People were always getting us mixed up,' stated Roland, accepting the tea. 'When we were younger we used to play tricks on the teachers, since they couldn't tell us apart.'

'You even sound like him,' said Mrs Pine, wonderingly.

'We were quite different in some ways though,' said Roland, with a smile.

'Oh, in what way?' demanded his interested listener.

'Let's say that John was always prepared to see the better side of human nature. I think I'm more of a realist.'

'It was believing in the best side of human nature that got him killed in the end,' said Mrs Pine, vehemently.

'You just said he'd died in the telegram you sent me,' said Roland. 'How exactly did it happen?'

47

Mrs Pine related the details. 'They say he was killed by one of the Olsens,' she ended, bitterly.

'They live on the ranch John was visiting?'

'That's right. They're Norwegian. They've never mixed with us townsfolk.'

'What has the sheriff done about it?'

'Him? He's useless. He did take a posse to the Olsen ranch. But when Olsen and his two sons threatened them with their guns they turned tail and came back.'

His next question took her by surprise. 'Where is John buried?'

'In the churchyard. By the church he was preaching in. He only held one service there.'

Until then she had been discussing John as though he were some distant acquaintance. Now, the thought of his funeral brought the whole tragedy alive once more. She began to sniff.

'Don't upset yourself,' said Roland. 'I'll get the bastard who killed John. I owe him that.'

CHAPTER 10

The news that John Payne's twin brother Roland had arrived spread like wildfire through the town. Roland had accepted his brother's room in Mrs Pine's house. He had gone through the few personal belongings that John had left behind, but except for some clothes, a well-worn Bible, a few family photographs and about a hundred dollars in notes there was nothing else.

He was staring at the few belongings when Mrs Pine knocked and entered the bedroom.

'Not much for a man to leave behind, is it?'

For the first time since he had arrived there was emotion in his voice. His face was taut as he tried to keep the tension in check.

'You cared a lot for him,' ventured Mrs Pine.

'He was too good for this rotten old world,' said Roland, with sudden venom. 'Why did he always see the good side of people? Why didn't he see that there is more evil in the world than good?'

'I don't know,' replied Mrs Pine. 'But if there were more people in the world like your brother maybe there would be more good people than evil ones.'

When Roland left the house he made his way to the cemetery. He glanced at the church. Mrs Pine had informed him how the one service John had held had been the most successful in the church's short history.

The cemetery was neatly laid out and there was a woman attending one of the graves. When Roland approached her he saw that she was probably in her late twenties and definitely pretty.

She glanced up as he drew near. He saw the startled expression on her face.

'You must be Roland, John's brother,' she stated.

'You know who I am, but I'm afraid I don't know who you are,' he said, with a smile.

'I'm May Stanfield. Mrs Pine said that the resemblance is uncanny,' she added.

Roland glanced at the grave. It bore a simple cross. It said 'John Payne, preacher'.

'He was only twenty-six,' said Roland, with a stony face.

May stared at him. She said nothing. She sensed that there was more to come.

'He wanted to live just helping other people. And some bastard didn't give him a chance.'

She was shocked by the sudden outburst, but

she managed to keep her face impassive.

'I'm sorry,' said Roland, finally.

'There's nothing to be sorry about. You have every right to be angry. I felt the same way when my husband died. I keep asking myself why should he have gone, and left me on my own, when we should have had so many years in front of us.'

Roland glanced at her as if seeing her for the first time. At last he said, 'What's the sheriff doing about John's death?'

'Him? Nothing,' said May, scornfully. 'He took a posse to Olsen's ranch, but when Olsen and his two sons met them with guns, he turned tail and came back.'

'You don't sound as though you've got much faith in him,' said Roland, drily.

'He's worse than useless,' she retorted.

'So if he isn't going to find out what happened to John, who is?'

She shrugged. 'Moss Lampton, maybe.'

'Who's he?'

'He owns the big spread to the right. He hates Olsen because he's planted corn on the range and put up fences. It used to be an open range before Olsen came here a couple of years ago.'

'If the sheriff is so useless why do the townsfolk keep him on?'

'His brother is the town clerk.'

Roland smiled. 'I see.'

May stared at him. She tried to spot some differences between him and John. There was none. Well, maybe just one. John had had a friendly open smile. It was the smile of a person who wanted to be friends with the whole world. Roland's smile was more guarded.

'Is there anything else I should know about John's killing?' He nodded towards the grave.

'No. It's just that we thought we were going to have a preacher in the town for some time,' she said bitterly.

' "The Lord giveth and the Lord taketh away",' Roland quoted.

May stared after him curiously as he walked away.

CHAPTER 11

Len Childs rode out to the homesteaders' shacks. There were a score or so of them spaced out with their allotted land around them. Some of the shacks were run down while others were neat and had obviously been freshly painted. Around most of the shacks were rows of vegetables and in most cases some chickens and a few pigs.

A few of the homesteaders were tending their vegetables. They looked up when Childs approached.

'Hi,' he said. 'I'm Len Childs. I work for Moss Lampton.'

'We've heard of you,' said the nearest of the homesteaders. 'My name is Carl Plover. If you've got anything to say, you can say it to me.' He was a stocky, powerful man with arms like tree-trunks.

'Most of you homesteaders help with the harvesting of Olsen's corn,' stated Childs.

'Yes, we've been doing it for the past couple of

years,' said Plover. 'What about it?'

'Moss Lampton asks you not to help Olsen with his harvest this year.'

Plover roared with laughter. 'Well you can tell him that his request is refused. Olsen pays us for harvesting his corn. With the money we stack up with provisions for the winter.'

'Moss Lampton is willing to pay you for not working on Olsen's ranch,' announced Childs.

'How much?' demanded a thin man named Kendal who had materialized by Plover's side.

'Twenty dollars a head,' said Childs.

'Twenty dollars.' Plover laughed. 'We can earn fifty dollars by helping Olsen get in his corn.'

'Twenty dollars is all Moss Lampton is willing to pay. You'd better think about it.' Until that moment his voice had been persuasive, now there was a hint of a threat in it.

'We can't decide this on our own,' said Kendal.

'That's reasonable,' said Childs. 'I'll call back at the same time tomorrow. I'll expect your answer then.'

At about the same time Roland was visiting the sheriff. He knocked and entered the office.

'I've been expecting you,' said the sheriff. He looked appraisingly at Roland. 'You're as like as two peas in a pod.' He emphasized the remark by spitting accurately into a spittoon.

'I want to know about finding my brother's

killer,' demanded Roland.

'We're pretty sure he's one of the Olsens,' replied the sheriff. 'Only we don't know which one.'

'Why should one of them want to kill John?' persisted Roland.

'We don't know. It just doesn't make sense.'

'Have you had any of them in for questioning?'

'How can I get them in for questioning?' There was a whining note in the sheriff's voice. 'The bastards threatened us with their guns the last time I took a posse to the ranch.'

'So what are you going to do?' Roland was getting angry.

'We'll just wait and see,' replied the sheriff. 'Sometimes you've got to give them enough rope and they'll hang themselves. I see you're wearing guns,' he added.

'I don't intend to get shot in the back the same way that John did,' retorted Roland.

After he left the sheriff's office Roland decided that he needed a drink. The sheriff's last remark and his obvious reluctance to act decisively was sticking in his craw.

He went into a saloon named the Buffalo's Horns. The bar was almost empty since it was too early in the day for most of the regulars to have put in an appearance. There was only a tall, thin young man standing by the bar and a group of card-players sitting at a corner table.

The barman, a middle-aged, red-faced man, who looked as though he was well acquainted with the spirits he sold, nodded to Roland.

'What can I get you?' he demanded.

'I'll have a beer,' stated Roland. He glanced across at the other occupant of the bar, but he was morosely staring at his glass and didn't appear to be the right person to ask to join him in a drink. Roland compromised by telling the barkeeper to have a drink himself.

'Thanks,' said the barman, pouring himself a generous measure of whiskey.

Roland was mildly surprised that the barman hadn't recognized him as John's twin. All the others he had met had done so. Then he reasoned that John would never have come inside a saloon – he had been a teetotaller. Hence the lack of recognition.

John was half-way through drinking his beer, when the young man at the far end of the bar shouted, 'It's you.'

Thinking that here was somebody who had recognized him Roland turned to face him.

The young man had gone pale and was obvious struggling with some inner emotion.

'You've come to haunt me,' he cried.

'Take it easy, Mr Olsen,' said the bartender.

So this was one of the Olsen family. It must be one of the two sons whom Mrs Pine had told him about.

Olsen was standing away from the bar. He had a wild expression on his face.

'You're not going to beat me,' he cried. ' I got rid of you once before. I'm going to get rid of you this time once and for all.'

What was he saying? Was he saying that he had killed John?

Olsen made a move which Roland always hoped he would never see. He went for his gun.

'You've made a mistake,' cried Roland. 'I'm not John.'

By now the other's gun had almost cleared his holster. Roland knew he had no choice. He drew his gun and fired a split second before Nils Olsen. Olsen fell to the floor in a pool of blood.

CHAPTER 12

Nils Olsen's funeral service was almost as well attended as John Payne's had been. Only this time the townsfolk turned out for sheer curiosity, not out of respect for the dead person.

The townsfolk were surprised on several counts. In the first place, at the number of the Olsen family who attended the church. The general impression had been that there were only the father, two sons and a daughter at the Olsen ranch. But here at the service there were quite a few other members of the family. In fact Mrs Pine counted fourteen in all. They say they have come from all over the county, she had informed Roland.

Another surprise was that they had even supplied their own preacher. He was a big man with a white beard.

'They say he's Nils's uncle,' supplied Mrs Pine.

Roland gazed at the members of the Olsen family who had all seated themselves at a side bench near the altar. He knew they were covertly gazing at him as the person responsible for this funeral service. In fact there was one exception to these surreptitious glances. It was the young woman who was sitting on the end of the bench. She was the most beautiful woman Roland had ever seen.

She was a blonde with the high cheekbones some Scandinavian woman have. She had a beautiful cupid's bow mouth. At the moment it was twisted into an expression of undiluted hatred.

The congregation had sung the opening hymn and the preacher went into his oration.

'We are gathered here to celebrate the life of Nils Olsen. Yes, celebrate, because, since Nils only lived for twenty-six years before he was cruelly taken away from his family, during those twenty-six years he had lived a happy life. But while we can celebrate Nils's life we must deeply sympathize with his family, particularly his father, his brother Sven, and his sister, Hedda.'

At the sound of her name she turned her gaze away from Roland. She began to sob silently into a handkerchief. At that moment Roland would have given anything not to have killed her brother.

The service drew to a close at last. Roland was among the first to leave the church. He didn't particularly want to come face to face with any of the Olsens although his conscience was clear. The sheriff had questioned him about the killing. The four card-players and the barman had seen the whole episode. They had testified that Nils Olsen had drawn first.

In fact the barman had said that Nils had already drawn his gun when Roland had started to draw. 'I've never seen anyone draw a gun so quickly in all the twenty years I've been behind a bar,' he had stated.

So he had signed a statement. He had been discharged.

'You got the feller who shot your brother,' the sheriff had informed him. 'It's good to see that it's over.'

Roland couldn't help reflecting that it had saved the sheriff a great deal of effort. He no longer had to go back to the Olsen ranch to arrest Nils.

He found himself in the cemetery. People were leaving the church. He walked over to his brother's grave.

He stared at the bunch of primroses that May had put on the grave. They looked as though they needed fresh water. He picked up the vase to carry it to the pump when he was aware of someone behind him. He turned.

It was Hedda. The expression of hatred which had been on her face had been replaced by anger.

'What gave you the right to kill my brother?' she blazed.

'He drew first. There were witnesses,' he countered.

'You could have wounded him. There was no need to kill him. If you'd wounded him, I would have looked after him.'

'I'm sorry. He was wild. I don't think he knew what he was saying. I think he thought I was my brother's ghost.'

'You're a gunslinger. You could have just wounded him,' she half-sobbed.

'I'm not a gunslinger. Listen, I'd have given anything not to have had to kill him. I couldn't just wound him because I'm sure he'd have shot me. He looked so wild. He said, I'm going to get rid of you, once and for all.'

'You think you've avenged your brother's killing, don't you?' she sneered.

'I'm sorry it had to end like this. But yes, I think I have avenged John's killing.'

'Nils was all right when we were in the old country. It was only when we came here that he started having those headaches.' She turned on her heel and started to walk away.

Roland stared after the beautiful Hedda, wondering whether she would ever forgive him for killing Nils.

CHAPTER 13

The following day a young messenger arrived at Mrs Pine's house. He left a message that the sheriff wanted to see Mr Payne.

Roland turned up at the sheriff's office about half an hour later. He went in and was met by the usual sight of the sheriff chewing tobacco.

'Sit down,' the sheriff said, indicating the only other chair in the office.

Roland waited for him to explain the purpose of his summons. To his surprise the sheriff began with a question.

'You haven't got a job, have you?'

'Not at the moment,' confessed Roland.

'Are you thinking of staying in Bircher?' asked the sheriff.

Where were these questions leading? He hadn't decided whether to stay or move on to another town.

'I'm not sure,' he replied.

'Suppose I offered you a job, would you think about it?'

'It depends on the job,' said Roland, with a smile.

'Deputy sheriff.' The other produced his ace with an accurate spit into the spittoon.

'I've never been a deputy sheriff before,' said Roland, warily.

'Some of the time you'd be in the office. Oh, not this office,' said the sheriff, seeing the look of reluctance on Roland's face. 'There's an office in the back. We could clean it up for you.'

'I don't know.' Roland stared thoughtfully out through the window. Bircher was a growing town. Maybe the sort of town where a man could put roots down. Maybe find the right woman and raise a family. Why did a mental picture of the beautiful Hedda come to him when he thought of this?

'You don't have to decide straight away,' said the sheriff, waving a magnanimous hand. 'Take a day or two to decide. As long as you let me know one way or another.' He spat to emphasize the point.

Roland went along Main Street. He half-decided to visit a saloon, then remembered what had happened the last time he went inside one. Instead he settled for a tea room.

Most of the tables were occupied by ladies. He was about to turn and forget about having a drink when a voice at a side table said:

'There's room at my table, Mr Payne.'

He turned. It was May Stanfield. She was indicating an empty chair opposite her.

'Thank you, Mrs Stanfield,' he replied, with a smile.

'You're welcome. And my name is May.'

'My name is Roland,' he stated, as he accepted the seat.

The waitress came round to take his order. She wanted to know whether he wanted lemonade or tea. He ordered a cup of tea. May was gazing at him appraisingly.

'What else could I order, coming as I do from Boston?'

May smiled. 'I bet you've used that line on ladies before.'

'Why is it that I feel you can see right through me?' he demanded, as he sipped his tea.

'Maybe because I've already seen the other side of you.' She couldn't keep the sadness out of her voice.

'You mean John? Yes, he was a far far better man than I will ever be.' He stared into his cup, morosely.

'You shouldn't keep comparing yourself with him.' She had automatically put her hand over his.

'No, you're right.' He brightened. 'Anyhow, while I'm here maybe you can give me some advice.'

'What is it?'

'The sheriff has offered me the post of deputy sheriff. Should I take it?'

'Oh, my God!' she said, withdrawing her hand. Her face had become white.

'What's the matter?' He was alarmed. 'Is there something wrong?'

'Your brother sat in that chair less than a month ago and said that he had been offered the post of preacher.'

'And you advised him to take it,' said Roland, with sudden insight.

'Exactly. And look what happened to him.' She was becoming agitated.

'The fact that he was shot had nothing to do with you,' he said slowly and persuasively. This time he had taken her hand. 'You must believe that.'

Two ladies at a nearby table were listening to the discussion with interest. They had not missed the fact that Roland and May had been holding hands from time to time.

She shook her head as though to banish any guilty thoughts. Her fair curls danced as she did so. Roland stared steadily at her.

'Feeling better?'

'Yes, I think so.' She managed a smile.

He withdrew his hand.

'So what's your advice?'

She swallowed. She knew what she had to say,

yet why was it so difficult?

'We'd love you to stay,' she said, quietly. So quietly in fact that the two ladies didn't catch it although they were straining their ears.

'That's settled then,' said Roland, with a smile.

CHAPTER 14

Roland, having accepted the post of deputy, was duly sworn in. To emphasize the seriousness of the position he was offering Roland, the sheriff even stopped chewing tobacco for the ceremony.

'You are now officially a deputy,' said the sheriff, pinning the star on Roland's shirt.

'What do I do first?' demanded Roland.

'Go and sort out the trouble between the Olsens and Moss Lampton. I've heard a rumour that Moss Lampton is trying to get the homesteaders not to cut Olsen's corn.'

'Is that serious?' demanded Roland.

'It is for the Olsens. If they don't get their corn gathered in soon they will lose most of it.'

'I assume it's ripe now for harvesting,' ventured Roland.

'Of course it is. You city folk don't know anything about the country,' smiled the sheriff, showing black and broken teeth.

Roland rather liked the idea of visiting the Olsens. Maybe he would even come across Hedda. Regretfully he knew though that he should visit Moss Lampton first. After all it looked as though he was the cause of the rift between the two families.

The sheriff had supplied him with a horse. It was quite old and maintained a dignified gait as it took him to the Lampton ranch. Roland wondered what would happen if he ever tried to get the horse to burst into a gallop.

He dismounted under the watchful gaze of a couple of cowboys.

'Is Moss Lampton in?' he asked the nearest one.

'I'll go and see,' he replied.

When he had disappeared into the house, the second cowboy, Mallard, said, 'I hear you're fast with a gun.'

'Fairly,' said Roland.

'Your brother was fast,' supplied the other. 'He beat us all to the draw.'

'Yes, he was fast,' Roland agreed, sadly. 'We used to have contests and he nearly always beat me.'

Why was he revealing this to a stranger, he wondered. He was saved any further revelations by the return of the other cowboy.

'Mr Lampton will see you,' he announced. 'He's in the study.'

Moss Lampton stood up to shake hands with Roland when he entered. He introduced himself and Len Childs, who waved an acknowledging hand but did not rise from his chair. Roland formed the instant impression that Childs was not the sort of person you would wish to become too friendly with.

'You'll have a drink?' invited Lampton, indicating the bottle of whiskey and the glasses on a side table.

'Thanks.'

Lampton poured him a generous drink. 'I offered a drink to your brother on the one occasion he came here, but he refused,' said Lampton, handing the glass to Roland.

'I told him that the Lord turned the water into wine,' supplied Childs.

'I'm sure he already knew that,' said Roland, drily.

Childs stared at him through narrowed eyes. He seemed about to say something, then changed his mind and turned his attention to his glass of whiskey.

'I've come about this dispute between yourself and the Olsens,' stated Roland.

'Dispute!' Lampton's voice rose. 'It's more than a dispute. It's war.'

Roland was shocked by the vehemence in Lampton's voice and by his choice of words.

'Take it easy, Uncle,' said Childs, placatingly.

'You know the doctor said you mustn't get excited. It's bad for your heart.'

Lampton's face had certainly become red. The last thing Roland wanted to do was to bring on a heart attack. Still, having come out here he should try his best to find out more about the war, as Lampton called it, between himself and the Olsens.

'When did this – er – trouble – start?' He put the question, diffidently.

'Two years ago.' Lampton's answer came rapidly. 'When that bastard Olsen first came to Bircher.'

'And what caused it?'

'What caused it? I'll tell you what caused it.' Lampton was on his feet and shouting. 'He fenced in the open range, that's what caused it.'

Childs jumped up and stood by his uncle's side. 'I think you'd better go,' he snapped. 'Before you do any more damage.'

Roland stood reluctantly.

'I'm only trying to get at the facts,' he stated, as he walked towards the door.

'If you want the facts, ask the widow of Richard Stanfield,' Lampton shouted after him.

CHAPTER 15

Roland returned to the sheriff's office. He wanted answers to some questions. The first one he put to the sheriff was: 'What's the connection between May Stanfield's dead husband and the Olsens?'

The sheriff leaned back in his chair. 'Richard Stanfield was the lawyer who handled all the transfer of the land to the Olsens two years ago.'

'Why is Moss Lampton so incensed about the transfer?'

'Until the Olsens came on the scene it was all open range. Moss Lampton could graze his cattle wherever he pleased. Then Olsen came here and the next thing we knew he was fencing in his land.'

'What about the land that the Olsens fenced in? Was there anything special about it?'

The sheriff looked at him appraisingly. 'It's got the only river than runs into Bircher.'

'So Moss Lampton's cattle depend on the rain

to water the grass?'

'Exactly. As you know, we don't get too much rain here. They say that Lampton has had to sell off half his cattle because there isn't enough grazing for them.'

'And on top of that Olsen planted corn on his land,' said Roland, thoughtfully.

'Exactly. I think you've got the picture.' The sheriff looked as pleased as a teacher whose favourite pupil has just achieved maximum marks in a subject.

Roland stood up.

'Are you off to see the Olsens?' demanded the sheriff.

'No, I'm going to see May Stanfield,' replied Roland.

He found her house without any difficulty. It was a smart white house which had recently been painted. Roland stepped inside the porch and knocked at the door.

May opened the door. She greeted him with a welcoming smile.

'Roland, this is a pleasant surprise,' she said, stepping aside to let him enter the house.

Seated in a comfortable living-room he broached the subject of his visit. 'I want some information about the connection between your late husband and Mr Olsen.'

'And I thought you'd come just to see me,' she said, with a wry smile.

'Business before pleasure,' he replied.

She sighed. 'What do you want to know?'

'I've heard the story about how your husband arranged for the Olsens to buy their land. The obvious question is, why didn't Lampton buy the land in the first place? I gather his family was here generations before the Olsens arrived.'

'Richard never confided anything about his business dealings to me,' said May, brushing a stray curl from her forehead. 'Of course he had a partner, Brendon Newman. I don't think Richard would have completed a big deal like the Olsens' land without having advice from Newman. In fact Newman was the senior partner.'

'Where will I find Newman?' demanded Roland.

'In Crichton. Richard used to work here for a couple of days a week, then go to Crichton for the rest of the week. There wasn't enough work for a full-time lawyer here in Bircher.'

'So my next call is Crichton,' said Roland, thoughtfully.

'Will you have tea first?' she asked with a winning smile. 'I've also got some excellent pastries.'

Roland hesitated. He stared into her pale-blue eyes. They were the sort of eyes which made it difficult to refuse such a request.

'Why not?' he said, finally. 'Newman can wait for another hour or so.'

'If you're planning to go to Crichton you won't be able to travel there and back in a day,' May informed him as she was pouring the tea. 'Richard used to go on one day then come back the following day.'

While he was munching a jam tart, May ventured, 'I heard a piece of gossip in the market yesterday. I don't know whether you've heard it.'

'What is it?' demanded Roland with sudden interest.

'Some of the Olsens have stayed behind after the funeral – the younger ones. Apparently they're expecting a show-down with Moss Lampton.'

'I see,' said Roland, sipping his tea thoughtfully.

'If there's any shooting you'll be careful, won't you?' implored May. 'To lose one of your family is bad enough. But to lose two . . . .' she choked at the thought.

'It'll be all right. My middle name is Careful.'

She managed a smile. She watched him take his leave. There was still a worried frown on her face.

'By the way,' she said, 'when Richard was in Crichton he used to stay in the Dog and Whistle saloon. He used to say that it was a nice quiet place.'

CHAPTER 16

It was late when Roland arrived in Crichton, largely due to his one-paced mare. He knew he would have to put off seeing the lawyer until the following day. He rode down the high street. It was a bustling town, largely owing its prosperity to the fact that the railroad had progressed as far as Crichton from Adamsville about three years before.

He needed somewhere to stay the night. There were plenty of saloons to choose from, but he searched for the Dog and Whistle as recommended by May Stanfield.

When he eventually found it he had a shock. It was far from being the quiet backwater May had described. In fact it couldn't have been more the opposite. When he dismounted from his horse he was accosted by two prostitutes who were obviously touting for custom outside the saloon. The shock wasn't completely confined to Roland, since when they saw the star on his shirt they beat a hasty retreat.

He was undecided whether to try to find a quieter saloon, or stay the night in the one in front of him. It was obvious that Richard Stanfield had been deceiving May about staying in a quiet saloon. There might have been some other events he had been less than truthful about. He decided he would stay in the saloon in order possibly to find out more about May's husband.

The bar was crowded, there being a young singer giving a rendering of some popular songs on a makeshift stage in the corner. Roland finally attracted the barman's attention.

'What can I get for you, Deputy?' he demanded.

'I'd like a room for the night.'

'No problem,' replied the barman. He called a young Mexican boy over. 'Take the deputy up to room sixteen,' he commanded.

Roland found that the room was quite clean, with a fresh jug of water standing on the sideboard. He tipped the boy and received a wide grin of appreciation in return.

'Me, Carlos,' said the boy. 'If you need anything, girls, whiskey, songs, just ask me.'

'You look a bit young to be touting for customers for the girls,' observed Roland.

'You look a bit young to be a deputy sheriff,' answered Carlos. 'The deputy sheriff here is old and fat.' He made a graphic gesture with his hand to indicate how fat he was.

Roland smiled. As Carlos was about to leave he stopped him.

'What's this about songs?'

'For five cents I will ask Lorna to sing any song you would like.'

'I'll keep it in mind,' said Roland.

Whether the barman was impressed by his star or not Roland wasn't sure. However he asked for and was served a hot meal in a small back room in quick time. Afterwards he strolled into the bar.

Lorna was singing the plaintive: 'I'm a-heading for the last round-up'. Roland ordered a beer while she finished the song. Her rendition was greeted with raucous acclaim by a group of cowboys in the corner.

He turned away from the scene and concentrated on his beer. He had spotted at least half a dozen prostitutes in the bar. It seemed as though May's husband had indulged in some extra-marital activities while he was in Crichton. He could obviously have chosen a saloon where prostitutes were non-existent. Yet he had chosen this place every time he had come to Crichton.

A female voice behind him said,' Won't you buy me a drink, Mr Lawman?'

Roland turned. It was one of the prostitutes he had spotted. He was about to tell her curtly to

make herself scarce when an idea occurred to
him.

'All right. What'll you have?'

'A whiskey. A girl has to keep warm somehow.'

He ordered the whiskey. As he handed it to her
he took in her appearance. She was wearing a
skimpy dress which did little to conceal her
figure. It was quite a shapely figure. If she had
taken off one of the several layers of powder and
paint from her face she could be quite an attractive young lady.

'You like?' she asked, coyly, seeing that he had
eyed her.

'I want some information,' said Roland, ignoring her question.

'I should have guessed I wasn't going to get
something for nothing,' she said, bitterly.

'Have you been working here for over a year?'

'What's this? I'm not getting into trouble with
the law, am I?' she enquired, belligerently.

'Answer the question.'

'I've been working here a couple of years. And
I haven't been in trouble with the law.'

'You're not going to get in trouble with the law.
And anyhow I'm not from these parts.'

'I thought I hadn't seen you here before.' She
had moved close to him and was rubbing her leg
against his.

'Though if you don't behave yourself I'll probably take you to the town's sheriff's office.'

She moved away quickly as though she had been stung.

'What do you want to know?' she demanded, sulkily.

'There was a lawyer. His name was Richard Stanfield. He used to come here regularly, until he died about a year ago.'

'Yes, I used to know him. He was one of my regular customers. I heard that he died. He always used to pay well.'

'He used to come here every week. Would you see him every time he came here?'

'Of course. He used to say that his wife didn't understand him.' She finished her whiskey in one gulp. 'Was that information worth another drink?'

'I don't see why not.' He ordered another whiskey for her.

Later, in his room he went over the picture the prostitute had painted of Richard Stanfield. It was not a very favourable one. He had been cheating on May regularly. The thought came unbidden that if he'd been married to May he was sure he wouldn't have needed to look for the services of a prostitute.

CHAPTER 17

The following day Roland presented himself at the lawyer's office. BRENDON NEWMAN. LAWYER was written in large Gothic lettering on the door.

There was a young man seated at a desk in an outer office.

'What can I do for you, Deputy?' he demanded, pleasantly.

'I'd like to see Mr Newman.'

'Have you got an appointment?'

'No.'

'I'll see if he's free.'

He disappeared into an inner room. When he reappeared he nodded to Roland. 'Mr Newman will see you.'

Roland entered the lawyer's room. It was a lavishly appointed room with a mahogany desk, shelves of law books, a thick Persian carpet and leather-upholstered chairs. Newman stood up to shake hands with Roland.

'What can I do for you, Deputy?'

He was an Irishman who hadn't quite lost his original accent. He was a handsome man in his fifties with white hair. He wore an immaculate grey striped suit.

'I'd like some information,' replied Roland.

Newman waved him to a chair.

'Information about what?'

'About your ex-partner, Richard Stanfield.'

A slight frown crossed Newman's face. 'Richard died about a year ago.'

'I'm working in Bircher. I'm checking on the land deal Stanfield concluded with a man named Olsen.'

This time the frown on Newman's face was quite apparent. 'I seem to remember something about the deal. Although Richard concluded the whole matter himself.'

'The person questioning the legality of the deal is a rancher named Moss Lampton.'

'That's a serious accusation to make.' Newman's mask of urbanity had slipped. In its place was raw anger.

'I assume you have all the documents relating to the land exchange.'

'Certainly.'

'Can I see them?'

'No, you cannot.' Newman thumped his desk, angrily. 'The only way you can see them is by court order. You'll have to see the town sheriff.'

Roland left the lawyer's office with a bad taste in his mouth. Did Newman have something to hide regarding the exchange of land? Was that why he had refused to let him see the transfer deed?

Well, the only way he could find out was to see the town sheriff. He found the office without any difficulty. He knocked and entered.

The sheriff's office too was well appointed though without the thick carpet of the lawyer's office. The sheriff, a bald-headed, middle-aged man, waved Roland to a chair.

Roland explained his request. The sheriff regarded him quizzically.

'So you think there might be something underhand about the land deal?'

'Moss Lampton does. It certainly seemed suspicious how somebody can arrive in Bircher from Norway and fence in part of the open range which has been free land for at least a hundred years.'

'It certainly raises some questions,' said the sheriff, thoughtfully.

Roland was pleased that he was dealing with a reasonable man after Newman's evasiveness.

'Newman told me that I would have to get a court order to see the transfer deeds.'

'That's right. It's no problem. I'll see the town clerk. If you'll call back this afternoon I'll have the clearance for you.'

Roland thanked him. He left the office in a happy frame of mind.

His happiness would have been shattered if he could have heard a conversation which took place in Newman's office shortly after he had left it. Newman had sent his clerk out to fetch a man named Styles. He knew he would find him in one of the saloons where Styles was playing cards.

'The boss wants to see you,' the clerk informed him.

Styles was dressed in black. Not that he was an undertaker. Although he had certainly helped to provide the undertaker with some considerable business over the years. Styles was a gunslinger.

He arrived in Newman's office.

'See that I'm not disturbed,' Newman instructed the clerk.

'What did you want to see me about?' demanded Styles. He sat in one of the easy-chairs and put his feet on another.

Newman controlled his annoyance at Styles's deliberate gesture of rudeness. He knew that Styles was a difficult person to deal with and one false move would jeopardize his whole plan.

'You know I've been busy controlling the land that the railway to Bircher will be built on?'

'The railway that will make you a millionaire,' sneered Styles.

'It will make you rich too,' Newman reminded him.

'What about it?' demanded Styles.

'There's a deputy sheriff from Bircher who's here asking too many questions. He could put a spanner in the works. All my years of planning could come to nothing.'

'What do you want me to do about him?'

'Kill him,' said Newman, calmly.

'Killing lawmen can come expensive,' said Styles, slyly.

'You'll have the usual payment. Plus a hundred dollars bonus.'

'Two hundred dollars,' stated Styles, emphatically.

Newman was about to argue. Then, realizing how all his plans depended on Styles killing the deputy sheriff, he reluctantly agreed.

'Where will I find him?' demanded Styles.

'He went to see the sheriff. I expect he's left by now. But he'll be going back there this afternoon to pick up some transfer deeds. I managed to stall him until then.'

'What's he look like?'

'He's a good-looking young feller. Fairly tall. Blond hair. He's wearing a green shirt with his badge on it.'

'I'm on my way,' said Styles, as he stood up.

'What about the deputy sheriff?'

'He's on his way, too. To Boot Hill.'

The two men burst out laughing.

CHAPTER 18

Several hours after Roland had set out on his journey to Crichton May Stanfield was still thinking about him. She was mildly irritated by the fact that he kept cropping up uninvited in her mind. She had to confess though that the mental picture she had of him was quite pleasing. He was undoubtedly a handsome man, as his twin John had been.

To begin with she had rather resented the fact that he had usurped his dead brother's place in her thoughts. It was as if somehow she was being unfaithful to John's memory. Not that there had ever been any hint of romance between herself and John. Indeed on the one occasion when she had invited John to tea he had made an unconvincing excuse not to come. It was just that he was the perfect man in all respects. As Shakespeare said in *Hamlet*, 'I shall not look upon his like again'.

Now here was Roland. He had killed a man. Everybody had said it was self-defence. She supposed that Roland was in a way more of a man's man. That didn't mean though that he lacked sensitivity. When they were talking together she could swear that sometimes they could read each other's thoughts. The last time they had sat here she had become quite upset at the thought that he might be putting his life in danger. She had been successful in managing to conceal it, but nevertheless the fear had stayed with her for ages after he had gone.

She realized she was pacing up and down the room. She must find something to do to stop her dwelling on the possibility of Roland being in danger. He had gone to Crichton to find out about the land deal with the Olsens. There were some papers in the attic that Richard had left behind. There was a faint possibility that there was a copy of the transfer deed among them. Richard had always been a careful man. In fact in her opinion he had been too careful. He had always been too . . . predictable, yes, that was the word. Sometimes she had longed for him to do or say something completely out of character. She would have liked them to have ridden off across the prairie together on two fast horses. They would have stopped by a secluded spot and made love. It could have been perfect.

Richard would never have dreamed of such an

adventure. It could have added a new dimension to their predictable existence. Would Roland ever have contemplated such a venture? He had a certain wildness about him which hinted that he might do so. What would it be like to be made love to by Roland?

She angrily rejected the thought. She made her way up into the attic. By the light of the oil-lamp she discovered that there was a trunk which was full of copies of deeds, wills and other legal documents. She sat down on the floor and began to go through them.

She discovered that far from being a boring task, she soon became fascinated by some of the papers. Some of the wills particularly held her interest. In fact time flew and she realized it was that time in the afternoon when she usually went to the café to have a chat with the ladies of the town. She regretfully put the papers which she had read to one side. She would have to leave the remainder for tomorrow.

In fact it was quite early in the morning when she began her self-appointed task of trying to track down the copy of Olsen's transfer deed. She was sure now that it was somewhere among the pile to be searched through. It was obvious that Richard had kept a copy of all his important transactions. They were even numbered, with the dates written legibly on them.

It was late in the morning when she found it.

She could hardly contain her excitement as she held it up to the lamp. If she had realized that a copy of the document was here in the attic there would have been no need for Roland to go to Crichton to find it.

She studied it. Her first impression was complete and utter disbelief. Her mind almost refused to accept what she was reading. But there was no doubt about it. Olsen had purchased the land for a hundred dollars. He had purchased 1,000 acres for a hundred dollars. It should have been worth at least a hundred times that amount.

More than that there was a clause stating that whenever Newman and Stanfield, lawyers, wished to purchase the land back they would do so. The original one hundred dollars would be refunded to the Olsens. They would give the Olsens three months to quit the land.

May sat on her heels staring at the document. What a weird clause. It had been sealed and witnessed and therefore it was obviously legal. What was behind it?

She racked her brains. The only thing she could think of was that the railway was coming to Bircher. It would be going through the Olsens' land. Anyone who owned it would make a fortune.

Wait a minute! The land wouldn't be owned by the Olsens when the railway was being built. It would be owned by Newman and Stanfield. Or rather Newman, since the Stanfield side of the partnership was deceased. What a perfect way to make a fortune. Newman would make tens of thousands of dollars by leasing his land to the railway company.

Was it legal, that was the question. She stood up and prepared to carry the revealing document down to the living-room. When she arrived there she read it once more. The fact that she was reading it in the daylight instead of by lamplight hadn't changed it one bit. She knew instinctively that there was something crooked about it. She had never trusted Newman and she knew that he would have been the brains behind it. Richard would never have thought up something as devious as this, though Richard must have gone along with the scheme in the first place.

Well, there was nothing she could do about it now. She guessed that Roland would discover the original deeds when he visited Newman's office in Crichton. It would certainly be interesting for them to compare notes when he returned to Bircher. She couldn't wait for his return.

'Oh, no?' prompted a cynical inner voice.

'It's only because I want to discuss the matter with him,' she told herself, angrily. 'What other possible reason could there be?'

'I wonder,' said the inner voice.

CHAPTER 19

Roland collected the release document from the sheriff's office in the afternoon as arranged. He would have time to see the original deed before the lawyer closed his office. Whether there was anything unusual about it would remain to be seen.

The sidewalk was fairly crowded, mostly with women, some of whom had been shopping. Others were accompanied by small children and Roland guessed that they had been collected from school and were on their way home.

He didn't spot the man dressed in black who was walking parallel with him on the opposite sidewalk. Styles had chosen that method of stalking Roland since he had reasoned that he had a better chance of killing him by shooting across the street. He had considered following Roland from behind and shooting him in the back, but had rejected the idea. There were too many women on the sidewalk and he couldn't guarantee having the chance to get a clear shot at Roland before he reached Newman's office.

Roland was walking on the edge of the sidewalk to avoid the women and this fitted in perfectly with Styles's plan. The only slight problem was that there were occasional riders passing along the road who obscured his vision for a few moments until they had passed. However once they had gone Roland was always easy to spot. For one thing he was taller than most of the other people on the sidewalk. For another he was wearing a distinctive green shirt with a star on it.

They had now reached a spot where the lawyer's office was visible in the distance. Styles knew that the moment to put his plan into action had almost arrived. There was a lane leading off to the left where he could make his escape after shooting the lawman. He would be away from the scene of the killing before anyone realized what had happened.

Roland, oblivious of the danger, was strolling casually along the sidewalk. Now and again he would step aside to avoid a mother and child. Some of the mothers cast wondering glances in his direction – he was obviously a stranger in town. Some of the young mothers cast appreciative glances in the direction of the good-looking lawman.

Suddenly there was a shout from behind Roland.

'Hey! Mister Marshal. Did you want any of the things I told you about? Girls, whiskey, songs?'

It was Carlos. Roland turned. In that split second he saw that the man in black on the sidewalk opposite was in the act of drawing his gun. Roland's reaction was instinctive. He drew his revolver with incredible rapidity. The two shots sounded as one.

Three days later Mrs Pine received a telegram. It was a rare occasion to receive one and usually signified a death. She opened it with trembling fingers. When she read it her trembling increased.

She knew she had to share the terrible news with somebody. It was too distressing to keep to herself. Ten minutes later she was knocking at May Stanfield's front door.

'I've just had a telegram. It's about Roland,' she gasped.

May paled. 'You'd better come in.'

Mrs Pine handed her the telegram. It was from the sheriff of Crichton. It said simply, 'I regret to inform you that the deputy sheriff, Roland Payne, has been shot. He is in a critical condition.'

May collapsed into an armchair.

'Shall I make us some coffee?' suggested Mrs Pine.

'Yes, please,' answered May, automatically.

While Mrs Pine was making the coffee, May reread the telegram. It had been sent three days before. The telegraph service was notoriously slow. In those three days anything could have happened. Roland could even have died. Oh, no!

She wasn't aware that she had groaned aloud until a concerned Mrs Pine appeared from the kitchen.

'Are you all right, May?'

May nodded, dumbly.

Mrs Pine brought in the coffee. They sipped it in silence.

'I suppose somebody should reply to the telegram,' suggested Mrs Pine.

'I'll do it,' said May, decisively.

After Mrs Pine had left May's thoughts were still in a turmoil. Was Roland dead or not? Was he seriously injured? The telegram hadn't said much. She had promised Mrs Pine to send a telegram in reply. But by the time they received the telegram Roland could be dead and buried. She grew cold at the thought.

She was pacing agitatedly about the room. What could she do? The stage wouldn't be leaving for Crichton until the end of the week. That would mean another delay of three days.

As she paced around the room a thought sprung up unbidden. At first she pushed it aside angrily. But it persisted and surfaced again. It seemed so preposterous that it wasn't even worth considering. Finally, though, she was forced to examine it.

She had a horse. A fast horse. She would have the whole day to ride to Crichton. She would arrive there before nightfall. She could find out what had happened to her Roland.

What was she thinking about, referring to him as 'her' Roland? He couldn't mean much to her, since she hadn't known him for long.

'Oh, no,' said an inner cynical voice.

CHAPTER 20

Len Burns, sheriff of Crichton, was a worried man. Usually, as his wife Emma would point out, he was not prone to worrying. He would generally take life as it came. True, in his job from time to time he came across occasions which would cause him momentary concern. These would be mostly confined to small fracas in the town – usually the result of some over-enthusiastic cowboys having had too much liquor in some saloon or other. Len's solution was invariably the same. He would hand the matter over to his deputy, Paul Dryden. Len had complete faith in him and knew with one hundred per cent certainty that Paul would deal with the matter, coolly and efficiently.

Paul Dryden was a comparatively young man, being in his late twenties while Len was in his late forties. Unlike Len, Paul wasn't married. This was the one black mark against him as far as Len was concerned. In every other way Paul was a perfect deputy. He could handle men in any given situation and his physical courage was never in doubt. However his relationships with women were never as successful. He was embarrassingly shy and while several young women in the town would have been happy to have gone out with him, since he was reasonably good-looking, they never had the opportunity. Paul hardly ever went to social functions, and when he did he would stand in the corner eagerly awaiting the event to conclude so that he could return home.

Now Paul had an unusual task. He was helping to look after a man who had been shot. Normally this responsibility would have been handed over to a doctor who would have found a nurse to take care of the wounded man, but this case was different. As the sheriff had explained, 'This guy, Roland Payne, is the deputy sheriff of Bircher. I think he was shot because he was on the trail of some crooked deal that the lawyer, Newman, was involved in. I think Newman was behind having him shot. If we hand Payne over to the doctor and he gives him to a nurse to take care of him, he would be in danger of the gunslinger shooting him again. This time he would make sure that Payne wouldn't live to cause any trouble.'

So for part of the day, Paul would find himself sitting in one of the sheriff's bedrooms, where the deputy was lying on the bed. Since the deputy was still unconscious there was nothing for him to do except to read some of the sheriff's books. Normally he wasn't a committed reader, but he found at least a few of the books were quite readable. Particularly those by the English author, Charles Dickens.

He was engrossed in the adventures of David Copperfield, when there was a knock at the door. Mrs Burns answered it. Paul immediately took up a position of alert readiness. He drew his revolver.

He could hear two female voices. At that he began to relax. He couldn't imagine that danger, if it would come, would come from a woman.

The conversation continued for some time. He couldn't distinguish any of it since the house was built of stone with thick walls which isolated any sounds.

Several minutes later there came the unmistakable sound of someone coming up the stairs. When May entered the bedroom with Mrs Burns she was surprised to see a lawman sitting by the bedside with a revolver in his hand.

'It's only a precaution,' explained Mrs Burns.

May's gaze flew to Roland. He looked so white and still. She was almost afraid to ask the question which was on the tip of her tongue.

'Will he live?' she finally stammered.

'The doctor says he has a good chance of pulling through,' stated Mrs Burns. 'He took two bullets out of him, but he's lost a lot of blood.'

'The bullets hadn't punctured his lungs,' explained Paul.

May glanced at him quizzically. Mrs Burns supplied the introductions.

May stepped closer to Roland. He looked so pale. She wanted to put out her hand and touch his brow.

'We'll wait downstairs,' said Mrs Burns. She was a matronly woman who had brought up three daughters and she knew exactly what May must be feeling, judging by her distraught expression.

When the two had left the room May stared at Roland. The strain of the long ride and of finding him at death's door suddenly proved too much for her. She flung herself down on the bed. Downstairs Mrs Burns, who had left the bedroom door open, could hear her sobbing.

'It's the best thing for her,' she informed a puzzled Paul.

CHAPTER 21

Newman and Styles were sitting in a bar in one of the quieter saloons in the town.

Newman was livid with anger. 'You missed him,' he hissed.

'It couldn't be helped. He moved at the last moment. Some young boy called him and he turned round. It put me off my shot.'

'It put you off your shot,' snarled Newman. 'Do you know what this has meant to me?'

'No,' admitted a rather subdued Styles.

'It mean I've got to close my office down until you finish off the job you should have done. I'll have to get out of town until you kill the deputy. That means I'll lose money. Because I'll be losing money I don't know whether I'll be able to pay you the sum we agreed.'

'I'll get him for you next time. I promise,' said Styles hurriedly.

Newman became a bit calmer. 'You'd better

make sure you do. Or the sheriff will be learning some interesting facts about you. Facts that will put you behind bars for the rest of your life.'

'Don't you threaten me.' It was Styles's turn to get angry.

It dawned on Newman that it wasn't a good idea to threaten Styles too much. The gunslinger had killed six men that he knew about. If pushed into a corner Newman would easily make it seven. The seventh being him.

Newman succeeded in putting a false smile on his face.

'There's no point in us quarrelling. We'll have another drink and go over the details of how you can make sure of killing the deputy sheriff.'

He signalled to the barman who brought over two more beers. When the barman had retired out of earshot Newman stated, 'The deputy is staying with the sheriff. That should make it easy for you to dispose of him.'

'Where does the sheriff live?' Styles enquired, as he sipped his beer.

'A little way out of town. On the road to Adamsville. There are half a dozen stone-built houses. You can't miss them. They're the only stone-built houses in the town.'

'How will I know which house he's in?'

'All the houses have names. The sheriff's house is called "Cartref".'

' "Cartref." That's a funny name.'

'Yes, it must be Mexican, or something. Anyhow you can't miss it. And this time make sure you don't miss the deputy,' he added, with more than a hint of menace.

Inside Cartref May had recovered her composure. The doctor had called and had informed her that Roland seemed to be recovering his strength.

'His pulse is almost back to normal and his heart is still strong,' he informed her, after hearing about her ride to Crichton to be with Roland. 'He should recover consciousness in a day or two.'

May and Emma had already become firm friends. Emma was hugely relieved to have another woman in the house who could help to watch over the deputy sheriff. The person who might have felt that he was the odd one out, Paul, had also accepted the situation placidly. In fact the arrangement suited him. The two women spent most of their time together, leaving him to his own devices. If he wanted to go outside to smoke a cigarette he could call on May to sit with the deputy. In the past he would have had to call on Emma. This he had often been reluctant to do, knowing that she was a busy housewife. But he had no qualms about calling on May, who would eagerly seize the opportunity of sitting with Roland.

It was on one of the occasions when he was outside idly smoking a cigarette that he caught sight of a movement in the bushes. Paul was a keen nature-watcher. He knew the names of all the birds in the locality. Some of the rarer ones he had watched for hours during his lonely walks in the hills. Like all nature-watchers he could spot an unusual movement among trees or bushes instantly. This ability now probably saved his life.

As soon as he spotted the movement he flung himself down on the ground. A bullet whizzing above his head told him that he had been correct in taking the action.

Although he was spread-eagled on the ground, Paul was not in such a precarious position as it might appear. The gunman was hidden in the bushes a couple of hundred yards away, that was true. But Paul knew roughly where he was hiding. To emphasize the point he sent a couple of bullets in the gunman's direction. One of them obviously found its target, since the arrival of the bullet was greeted with a yell of pain. Paul smiled grimly.

It did not take Paul long however to realize that they had reached a stalemate. It was obvious that the gunman had crouched lower into the bushes to avoid receiving another bullet from him. On the other hand if he moved as much as an inch he would reveal his exact position and would expect a bullet which would do more damage than make him yelp with pain. The situation was resolved from an unexpected source. Suddenly someone started shooting from the upstairs window.

It was from the bedroom where the deputy was lying ill in bed. For one ridiculous moment Paul imagined that the deputy must have recovered and was shooting at the gunman in the bushes. He didn't have time to examine the idea because the gunman, suddenly realizing that he was in a crossfire, dashed out of the bushes and headed for the road. It was then that Paul calmly shot him in the back.

From the way the gunman collapsed Paul knew that he would not need a second bullet. Afterwards everything was in a state of chaos. Paul went over to the man in black. He confirmed that he was dead. When May joined him Paul was being sick. Even in the midst of his stomach turmoil he realized that May was carrying a smoking gun.

'You shot at him from the bedroom,' he gasped in amazement.

'He's the person who shot Roland, isn't he?' demanded May, with a gleam in her eye.

'I'm pretty sure he is.'

'Then I'm glad I helped you to shoot him,' announced May, triumphantly.

There was one more surprise to come. When May went back up to the bedroom to return Roland's gun to its holster, she was overcome with emotion at the sight that met her eyes. Roland was sitting up in bed.

CHAPTER 22

It was three weeks later when May and Roland returned to Bircher on the stage. May had insisted that they take the stage arguing that Roland was not yet strong enough to ride to Bircher. Roland had concurred with a wry smile. He had been riding for the past week and felt that the ride to Bircher wouldn't be too much of a problem. But May had been such a perfect nurse and companion in every respect during his convalescence that he felt he owed it to her to agree with her decision.

His recovery had been little short of a miracle according to the doctor. According to all the medical books Roland should have taken at least six weeks to recover from his loss of blood. Roland had replied that he put his recovery down to good food and good nursing. Mrs Burns had provided the food while May had supplied the nursing.

In point of fact May had never been so happy in her life. To see Roland gaining strength day by day was, as the doctor had said, a miracle. May had never been what she called a deeply religious person, but on her daily walk into town she would call in the church and offer up a silent prayer for Roland's salvation.

Roland, in fact, couldn't have found a more perfect companion during his convalescence. May was patient, attentive, witty and above all, intelligent.

'They seem a perfect couple,' Mrs Burns had remarked on more than one occasion to her husband.

'I know, my dear, so you've informed me several times,' said her husband, with a patient smile.

'There's only one thing I'd like to see before they go back to Bircher,' she persisted.

'What's that?'

'That he would propose to her.'

'You've been reading too many dime booklets,' retorted her husband.

Mrs Burns shook her head with annoyance. 'Oh, men!' she exclaimed exasperatedly.

The idea, too, had crossed May's mind. She and Roland were such perfect company for each other. They could spend hours together and yet the time flew as though they had only spent a few minutes together. She knew that if he suggested that they could get married she would jump at the idea.

But the suggestion never came. As they sat in the stagecoach on their way to Bircher May was forced to face the unpalatable truth. Roland was never going to ask her to marry him. The second realization she had to face up to was that perhaps he had a girlfriend in Boston. Maybe he had left somebody behind and would return to Boston once day to marry her. She sniffed involuntarily at the thought.

'Are you all right?' demanded Roland with concern.

'I think I might have a cold coming on,' she lied.

She reflected that it was strange, they had chattered so much when they had been in the sheriff's house in Crichton, and yet now, while they were in the stage they had little to say to each other. It was almost as if they were strangers. Of course the fact that there were two other travellers inhibited the conversation. These were a husband and wife. They were not a particularly attractive middle-aged couple. At any attempt at conversation by either Roland or May they would glare at the person as though they had committed some crime or other.

They eventually reached Bircher. It was with relief that they got out of the coach.

'Are you going to come in for a cup of coffee?' asked May.

'No, I think I'd better go to my lodgings,' he replied.

They stood together awkwardly. May knew that he had something else to say.

'I can't thank you enough for what you did . . .' he began.

'It was nothing,' she heard herself reply.

'I'll see you later,' he stated.

'You know where to find me,' she replied, turning on her heel and heading towards her cottage.

CHAPTER 23

The following morning Roland went to the sheriff's office. The sheriff looked up from his desk.

'You're back,' he said, unnecessarily. To celebrate the event he moved the chewing tobacco from one side of his mouth to the other.

As Roland sat in his chair he mentally compared the uncouth character sitting opposite him to Len Burns, sheriff of Crichton. Len was a civilized person with whom you could discuss a wide range of subjects. While the person sitting opposite him would have difficulty in expressing an opinion on any subject. In the first place he would have to remove his chewing tobacco, Roland decided humorously.

'There's been some trouble while you've been away,' announced the sheriff.

'What sort of trouble?' ventured Roland.

'Moss Lampton has brought some gunslingers into town.'

Roland wondered whether he should explain to the sheriff the land deal that the Crichton lawyer had agreed with the Olsens. In the end he decided against it.

'I'd better ride out and see if I can calm things down,' said Roland.

'You do that. Go and see Moss Lampton,' agreed the sheriff.

Roland set out. However he didn't go in the direction of the Lampton ranch, instead he swung his horse towards the Olsens' ranch.

It felt strange riding towards the ranch where his brother had been shot. He rode round the edge of the golden corn which swayed gently in the breeze. After riding for a few minutes he could see the Olsens' ranch in the distance.

As he neared it he could distinguish two men who appeared to be standing by the gate. On closer acquaintance he saw that they held guns in their hands. The guns were pointing at him as he approached.

'I've come to see Mr Olsen,' he shouted, stopping at a discreet distance away from the two gunmen.

'I'll see if he's prepared to see you,' said one of the gunmen.

He disappeared inside the house. After a while he reappeared.

'You can come in,' he announced.

A few minutes later Roland was sitting in the

living-room of the ranch. He was seated on one side of a long oak table. On the other side sat Mr Olsen, his son Sven and Hedda.

'Say what you have to say then go,' said Mr Olsen, uncompromisingly.

Roland sighed. He'd always known that this wasn't going to be easy.

'I've been to Crichton to see the lawyer, Newman,' he stated.

Mr Olsen's bushy eyebrows moved together in a frown. 'And?'

'I know all about the land deal that he arranged with you.'

The statement was obviously a minor bomb-shell.

'What deal?' demanded Sven.

'What's he talking about?' demanded an angry Hedda.

The thought flashed through Roland's mind, even when she's angry she's stunningly beautiful. He waited for her father's reply. It was a long time forthcoming. In the end Roland was forced to break the silence.

'Shall I tell them, or shall you?'

'You tell them,' growled the old man.

Roland addressed his remarks to Hedda and Sven.

'Your father agreed to go along with a deal concocted by a crooked lawyer, Newman, in Crichton. The deal was that your father would have the land to run as he wanted until Newman wanted to buy it back.'

'So we could lose the land,' said a shocked Sven.

'That isn't all,' said Roland. 'Your father only paid one hundred dollars for the land. When Newman wishes to close the deal that is all he'll get back.'

'But I thought you bought the land with the money Uncle Lange had left you,' protested Hedda.

The old man entered the discussion for the first time. 'Uncle Lange didn't leave me any money. He had gambled it all away.'

'So when this lawyer decides to end the contract we could end up with nothing.' Sven thumped the table in his anger.

'It might not happen for a few years,' said the old man, placatingly.

'It could happen sooner than you think,' supplied Roland. 'The deal depends on the railway that's coming from Crichton to Bircher. It's already reached about half-way between the towns.'

Hedda's next question took Roland by surprise. 'How do we know you're telling the truth?'

'Because I went to Crichton to find out.' Roland was surprised at the anger in his voice. 'I got shot for my pains. If you want to see the bullet marks, here they are.'

He rapidly stripped off his shirt and showed the two scars which the bullets had left behind.

'Put your shirt back on, young man,' said Mr Olsen, not unkindly. 'We believe you.'

'I'm sorry,' muttered Hedda, with a downcast face.

'Hedda, perhaps you'll make coffee for our guest,' suggested Mr Olsen.

While she was making coffee, Sven addressed a question to Roland.

'What do we do now?'

Roland felt it was a question he should be asking his father, but it showed his new-found status as a reliable adviser.

'There's no doubt that the deal will be concluded when Newman calls it in. The only thing in your favour is that at the moment Newman has disappeared.'

'What do you mean – disappeared?' Hedda reappeared with the coffee.

'He sent a gunslinger to finish me off before I scuppered his plans. The gunslinger was killed. Newman is lying low for a while.'

'So what do we do?' Hedda, too, addressed the question to Roland.

'Newman is bound to turn up sooner or later to complete his deal with the railway company. He stands to make tens of thousands of dollars. So we'll have to assume that he'll come to claim it.'

'What about him being behind the guy who

tried to kill you?' asked Sven.

'Newman is a clever lawyer. He'll manage to wriggle out of that. So there's one alternative left.'

'What's that?' demanded Hedda.

'You'll have to cut your losses. You've got hundreds of acres of corn out there. Get it in. It must be worth ten thousand dollars.'

'How do you know so much about the price of corn?' demanded Mr Olsen, suddenly taking part in the discussion.

'My uncle owned a corn-mill in Boston. I used to work for him.'

'You used to live in Boston?' There was a hint of envy in Hedda's voice.

'Yes, until my uncle lost all he owned. He was a gambler.'

A smile flitted across Hedda's lips. The suggestion of a look of admiration with which Roland regarded her was not lost on her father.

'There's only one problem,' put in Sven.

'What is it?' demanded Roland.

'Moss Lampton has paid the homesteaders not to cut our corn.'

'Is that true?' Roland addressed the question to Hedda.

'Yes, Daddy has been over to see the homesteaders on two occasions. They say that Moss Lampton has threatened to let his gunslingers loose on them if they cut our corn.'

'Can't you get some helpers from the town?'

'I'd want fifty. They'd have to be used to handling a scythe. It would be impossible to get enough men.'

The three of them were looking at Roland expectantly. The only one, though, whom he saw was Hedda. The look of expectation in her eyes was enough to make most men jump on their charger and dash off to seek help. In Roland's case he jumped on his one-paced horse, after promising to call to see the homesteaders.

CHAPTER 24

Roland rode slowly out to the homesteaders' shacks. He saw from a distance that many of the homesteaders were busy working their plots of land. As he neared he saw that several of them had raised their heads and were watching his approach.

When he was within speaking distance a thick-set man greeted him.

'Hi!' Plover waved a friendly hand.

'I've come to see about you guys working for Mr Olsen,' stated Roland, drawing up his horse opposite him.

'I'm afraid there's a bit of a dispute about it,' stated Plover, squinting up at him. Several other homesteaders had now gathered round. They were regarding Roland expectantly.

'Olsen needs you to get his corn in.' Roland

realized that he was shouting.

'We've been warned off helping Olsen get his corn in,' said Kendal, who was standing near Plover. 'He's paying us twenty dollars each not to help with the corn.'

'How much would you be getting if you helped Olsen get in his corn?'

'Fifty dollars.'

Roland surveyed the sea of faces which had now gathered around him. 'If I can get Moss Lampton to change his mind will you all work for Olsen as usual?'

There was a chorus of assent.

'Right, I'll be back,' stated Roland, turning his horse and heading towards the Lampton ranch.

As he neared it he could see the usual group of cowboys gathered outside the ranch. They don't seem to be too busy with their work, he thought as he approached. Mallard was one of those watching his approach.

'Hi, Deputy,' he said.

Roland wondered why he felt slightly apprehensive, even though the dozen or so cowboys who had gathered around him appeared friendly enough on the surface.

'Is Mr Lampton in?' he demanded.

'Haven't you heard?' said Mallard.

'Heard what?' asked a puzzled Roland.

'Mr Lampton had a stroke yesterday. It's a serious one. He's completely paralysed.'

'So I'm in charge now,' said a voice from the doorway. Roland glanced over to find out its owner. It was Childs. Although he was merely standing in the doorway there was something slightly menacing in his attitude. Roland noticed that he was wearing guns.

'In that case I want to talk to you,' said Roland, evenly.

'You'd better come in,' said Childs.

A couple of minutes later they were seated in the study where Roland had sat when Moss Lampton had last welcomed him to the ranch.

'I'm sorry to hear about your uncle,' said Roland. 'Is there any hope of him recovering soon?'

'The doctor doesn't seem to think so,' replied Childs, watching him closely. 'He thinks he might not last more than a few days.'

If Roland was expecting some hint of sadness in Childs's voice he was mistaken. Childs had made the statement much as he might have been reporting about the loss of one of the cattle out on the range.

'I see. Then I suppose the matter I've come about I'll have to discuss with you.' He managed to keep his dislike of the person seated opposite him out of his voice.

'That's right. I'm in charge now.'

'The homesteaders want the threat of working for Olsen lifted. They can get his corn in

127

and they'll be paid about fifty dollars for doing it.'

'You can tell them that the offer has been changed.' There was a smirk of triumph on Childs's face.

'So they can go ahead and help him get in his corn?'

'No. The thing that has changed is that we will no longer be paying them twenty dollars for not gathering in the corn.'

'So they can go ahead and gather it in?' Even as he put the question Roland guessed the answer.

'Of course. If they want to. The only thing is that there might be some accidents on their land while they're away. You know the sort of thing. Livestock getting stolen. Crops getting trampled on by cattle.'

Roland flared up. 'You bastard.'

'Nobody calls me a bastard and gets away with it,' snarled Childs. 'Maybe you'd like to put your gun where your mouth is, Deputy?'

Roland hesitated for a fraction of a second. A few weeks ago he wouldn't have hesitated in taking up Childs's challenge. But since being shot he knew he hadn't recovered fully. His reactions were not as quick as they were. He hadn't even practised drawing a gun for weeks. While on the other hand it was a safe bet that Childs practised daily.

Roland stood up. 'You won't get away with this,

Childs,' was his parting shot. But it was nauseating to see the gloating expression on Childs's face.

CHAPTER 25

Still smarting from the humiliation of not accepting Childs's invitation to draw, Roland rode slowly back to Bircher. He knew he had to report to the sheriff the failure of his mission.

In his report Roland cut out the fact that Childs had challenged him to a gunfight but that he had refused. When he had finished he said, 'So unless Olsen manages to get some help to cut his corn he could lose most of it.'

The sheriff's reply took him by surprise. 'That's the best thing that could happen. Maybe then he'd go back where he came from. Ever since he came here a couple of years back there's been trouble.'

'He's only growing corn,' retorted Roland, hotly. 'You want bread, don't you?'

'What's that got to do with it?'

'Everything.' Roland was on his feet and shouting now. 'We're supposed to be creating a multicultural society and here you are condemning Olsen because he's Norwegian.'

'I won't be shouted at in my office,' snapped the sheriff.

'You mean you won't listen to the truth in your office,' snapped Roland.

'Maybe you should have stayed in Boston where your ideas are accepted,' spat out the sheriff.

'Maybe I should have,' said Roland, drawing a weary hand over his brow. For a moment he considered handing in his badge. But that would mean running away from the situation. It would mean leaving the Olsens at the mercy of Childs. And by implication it would mean deserting Hedda also.

The sheriff was regarding him with a fixed expression. At last he said, 'I think you'd better go home. If you ask me you've come back to work too soon. You've not got over the bullets you had.'

Roland was surprised at the show of compassion. 'Maybe you're right,' he stated. 'I'm sorry I shouted,' he added.

'Take a few more days off,' advised the sheriff. 'Go for a ride with the widow Mrs Stanfield,' he added, with the nearest expression to a smile that Roland had seen on his face.

In fact May was busy struggling in the arms of a man named Quince. It had all happened so suddenly and unexpectedly.

About half an hour before there had been a knock at the door of her cottage. She had opened it. The shock of seeing her dead husband's partner and a half-caste standing there was compounded when he pushed past her into the house.

'What do you want?' she stammered.

'A few moments of your time, May,' said Newman, making himself comfortable in the easy chair.

'Say what you've got to say and get out,' she said, having recovered her composure. 'And don't call me May.'

'If you want to keep it on a business footing that's all right by me.' Newman drew out a thin cigar from a pack and proceeded to light it.

'So what do you want?' demanded May. She couldn't help glancing at the half-caste who was standing impassively by the door.

'His name's Quince,' said Newman, conversationally, as he lit the cigar. 'But it's no good you calling him by it, since he's deaf and dumb.'

'All right, say what you've got to say then you and your bodyguard can get out.' She sounded more confident than she felt as she uttered the words.

'We've just come for your signature on a document,' said Newman, smoothly.

'On what document?' demanded a puzzled May.

'Let me explain,' said Newman, putting his fingers together like a teacher in front of a class. 'Now that you know about your late husband's and my little venture into the field of property-buying things have become a little complicated.'

There wasn't any threat in his words, was there? May hastily dismissed the thought.

'You see,' continued Newman. 'Since your husband was dead and you had no knowledge of the transaction, you didn't present any threat.'

What did he mean, threat? She found that her mouth had unaccountably become dry.

'But now, since you obviously know about the deal, things have changed.'

'In what way?' gasped May.

'Ah, you did know about the deal,' said Newman, triumphantly. 'I had to confirm that before we proceed to the next step.'

Why did she have to keep glancing at Quince as though fascinated by him?

Newman, too, had observed her concern.

'He will not bother you unless I tell him to,' he assured her. 'He's only just come out of prison. He's quite docile unless I give the command.'

'What do you want?' That sounded quite confident, didn't it?

'I want your signature on a document,' stated Newman. 'It states that you have no further claim on the land deal that Richard and I concocted.'

'Richard would never have been involved in

working out such a scheme,' she said hotly.

'You loyalty to your ex-husband does you credit, my dear. But it is totally misplaced. Richard was involved in the scheme from the beginning.'

'I don't believe it.'

'I see that you are suffering under a misconception about your ex-husband,' said Newman, conversationally, taking a pull on his cigar. 'Did you know for instance that he had several mistresses.'

May put her hands to her ears. 'I don't want to listen to your lies,' she protested.

Newman reached over and pulled one of her hands away. 'When he stayed in Crichton he used to stay in a whorehouse named the Dog and Whistle.'

She listened in spite of her revulsion at his words.

'At least two of the whores were his regular girlfriends. They were quite upset when he died so suddenly.'

'It isn't true,' she whispered, half to herself.

'Oh, it's true, all right. You've only got to send a telegram to the saloon to confirm it.'

Why was he tormenting her? She'd sign his document and then he could get out of her life for ever.

'Where's the document?' she demanded, wearily.

'Here it is,' Newman unrolled it. 'If you will just sign here it states that you revoke any claim you had to the deal your husband and I drew up.'

She signed with an unsteady hand. 'Now you can get out,' she snapped.

He dried the signature carefully. When he was satisfied he put it away in his case.

'There's one thing I forgot to tell you,' he announced.

'What's that?' Her suspicion was aroused again.

'It's Quince. As I explained he's been in prison. During that time he hasn't had any female company. I promised him that if he came with me I could remedy that.'

'You bastard.' As quickly as the words were out her movement was almost as rapid. She shot towards the door leading into the kitchen.

For a man used to a sedentary life Newman moved with unexpected speed. He grabbed her arm. She struggled to release herself. Before she could do so Newman had handed her over to Quince. The struggle when she had attempted to get out of Newman's grasp was nothing compared to that which she was now involved in.

Quince had flung her down on to the floor. His foul breath almost made her vomit as he put his face to hers. She twisted her face away from him. Quince was feverishly scrabbling at her clothes. What about her neighbours? Would they hear her if she screamed? She made a sound which was more like a high-pitched squeak than a scream. Almost immediately she realized that she needed all her strength to try to fight off the madman who lying was on top of her.

He had torn off her dress and was struggling to get at her underclothes. She knew with a sickening certainty that there was nothing she could do about it. As they struggled they moved crablike around the floor. Quince had succeeded in tearing off some of her underclothes. She felt the cold air on her skin. Quince, although he was dumb, was making strange grunting noises in his throat. She scrabbled at his face with her hands, managing to scratch his face. He didn't even bother to try to move his head to avoid her fingernails.

She was sobbing as she realized that he had almost succeed in achieving his object. She tried to make one last determined effort to escape from his clutches, but he was too strong. Their struggle had brought them up against the grate. There was no fire in it but there was one faint possibility of her escaping her attacker. It was as faint as a drowning person grasping at a straw, but she had no choice. She grasped the tongs lying in the gate with her free hand. Quince had given another of his grunts at having finally divested her of almost all her clothes. He was about to achieve his desired objective when she drove the sharp tongs into the side of Quince's neck.

Afterwards everything happened so quickly. There was a knock at the door. May, having succeeded in escaping from Quince's grasp, shot towards it. She opened it and discovered Roland standing there. He took in the situation in a flash. Quince was coming towards him with a knife and the obvious intention of using it. Roland drew his gun with startling rapidity and shot him.

CHAPTER 26

Roland was riding like the wind. He was heading towards Crichton. He knew that Newman had about half an hour's lead on him, but it didn't decrease his determination to catch up with the crooked lawyer.

At last Roland was riding a fast horse, not the one-paced mare he had ridden in the past. It was May's horse which she had insisted he should take when he had made it clear that he intended to follow Newman, come what may.

The delay of half an hour or so had been necessary since he had spent most of that time comforting a tearful May. After ascertaining that Quince was indeed dead, he had taken her in his arms to comfort her. In point of fact it had been a pleasant experience, heightened by the fact that she was almost naked. He couldn't help observing that she was well-shaped – a fact that wasn't exactly apparent under the clothes she usually wore.

As he held her she gradually calmed down. They hadn't spoken since he had confirmed that Quince was indeed dead. Now she said, 'Thank you.'

'As long as you're all right, that's the main thing.'

She knew what he meant. 'Yes, I'm all right,' she assured him.

He was gently stroking her hair as he held her. She could have stayed like that for a long time. A very long time. She sighed and reluctantly drew away.

'Newman was out in the kitchen,' she stated. 'I heard him going after you came in. He was behind all this.' She explained exactly what Newman's involvement had been. Which was why he was on her horse heading towards Crichton.

There was no doubt in Roland's mind that that was where Newman was heading. The only question was whether the lawyer was expecting him to be following him. If he wasn't then he should catch up with his quarry long before he covered the eleven miles to Crichton. If, however, Newman had guessed that he would be on his tail then it would be a race to catch the lawyer before he reached the safety of Crichton.

Roland had no doubt that Newman would be safe once he reached Crichton. He could disappear into any of the twenty-two saloons in the town. He knew the exact number since the deputy, Paul, had informed him of the figure. He and Paul had spent many hours discussing various subjects while he was convalescing and the saloons and their various inhabitants had been one of those topics.

The other worrying thought was that if Newman reached Crichton say half an hour ahead of him he could have time to catch a train. Once on the train for Adamsville, Roland knew that he had less chance than the proverbial snowball in the hottest place of ever catching him.

Roland spurred his horse to greater effort. No, May's horse, he mentally corrected himself. There was no doubt she was quite a woman in all respects. He had first assumed she was a rather retiring young widow who spent most of her time involved with the church and the women's charities in Bircher. But during the past few weeks he had discovered an unexpected side to her nature. The fact that she had ridden to Crichton to nurse him was an act of charity far beyond any Christian teaching. The hours she had spent with him when he was convalescing he would always remember as some of the happiest days of his life. She had spent ages reading some of the classical books that the sheriff had in his house. She was an excellent reader who made the pages come alive. Occasionally they would discuss some character or event in the book. Sometimes they would disagree about something or other. If he won the argument she would flounce off in mock annoyance. Then invariably return with a cup of coffee. Yes, they had been happy times.

He was so wrapped up in reminiscing that for a few moments he didn't realize that Newman was in sight. Then, when he spotted the unmistakable figure of the lawyer, he could have whooped for joy. They were still three or four miles from Crichton. The odds were definitely in favour of his catching the lawyer.

He was succeeding in closing the distance between himself and his quarry. Whereas when he had spotted Newman the distance had been about a mile, now it was about a quarter of that distance. Newman was riding at a steady gallop. As they neared Crichton the scenery was changing. Whereas for the past few miles they had been riding though prairie which was uninhabited except for the occasional cattle, now they were coming to isolated farmhouses. There were farmers or cowboys riding their horses as they rounded up their cattle. It was at one of these isolated farms that Roland's plans to catch up with Newman before he was aware that he was being followed, went awry.

One of the farmers, who was out in the front of his farm tending to some livestock, called out to Newman.

'Howdy, Mr Newman.'

There was nothing unusual in that, thought

Roland. Newman had probably had some dealings with him in the past. It was what happened
next, however, that put the cat among the
pigeons. The farmer had spotted Roland coming
up fast behind the lawyer. Possibly not wishing to
favour one eminent member of the community
more than the other he called out:

'And howdy, Deputy.'

Newman instinctively turned. His next movement was equally instinctive. He spurred his
horse to shoot forward like a ball from a
cannon.

They were now racing each other. Newman
had a slight advantage since his horse, not
having been ridden hard, the way Roland had
ridden his, was rather fresher. The result was
the distance between them was gradually
increasing.

Roland had planned to take Newman alive. It
would be interesting to hear him try to wriggle
out of his crimes in a court of law. Now, though,
he was forced to change his mind. It was obvious
that Newman would reach Crichton before him if
he didn't alter his preconceived plan. His answer
was to draw his revolver and fire a couple of shots
at his quarry.

Although the shots didn't hit Newman, they
had an unexpected effect. The horse reared in
fright. The sudden movement threw Newman
from the saddle. Roland watched with grim satis-

faction as Newman scuttled to a dilapidated barn.

Roland's feeling of satisfaction at the fact that Newman was no longer escaping from him was tempered with reality when a couple of Newman's bullets almost singed his hair. Roland dived from his horse and took shelter on the other side of the barn.

They were about half a mile from the nearest occupied farm. There was no possibility of interference from outsiders. Roland accepted the fact as he carefully put his head round the corner of the barn. He was met with another couple of Newman's bullets, which came uncomfortably close.

Roland realized that he had to find a way of breaking the deadlock. He glanced inside the old barn. Whoever had abandoned the farm had left a quantity of straw inside it. He stared at the straw as an idea began to form.

Newman couldn't escape from the barn without dashing across a flat piece of land to reach his horse, which was now grazing unconcernedly after its initial fright. Roland decided to instigate that process by setting fire to the straw. After a few moments and only a slight wisp of smoke Roland wondered whether the straw was too wet to burn. He was on the point of changing his tactic and trying to force Newman out by shooting at him, when the flames caught. Soon they were crackling happily. Roland watched in eager anticipation.

In fact not only the straw but the whole barn was dry and ready for the flames. Soon they were licking upwards steadily. Roland had moved slightly away from the door. The fire had now reached the roof. It could only be a matter of time before the whole structure collapsed.

Newman had also realized the fact. He suddenly dashed out of the barn and headed for his horse. Roland took careful aim and fired. Newman collapsed on to the ground.

Roland approached him cautiously.

'You've shot me in the leg, you bastard,' yelled Newman.

Roland smiled grimly. As he approached Newman he said, 'Throw your guns away from you.'

Newman did as he was commanded. He was obviously in pain with the effort of tossing his guns away. Roland replaced his own guns in their holsters.

It was almost a fatal mistake. Newman produced a small gun from inside his jacket. Roland watched in disbelief at the completely unexpected action.

Whether the fact that the lawyer's leg, which was twisted uncomfortably under him, caused Newman to miss with his first shot, Roland would never be able to ascertain. What he was able to swear to, however, was that by the time Newman had tried to take aim a second time Roland had drawn his own gun in one lightning movement. He shot Newman between the eyes.

CHAPTER 27

Roland returned to Bircher the following day at a much slower pace than he had ridden to Crichton. In fact the only time he had slowed his horse down on the previous day was when he had ridden the last mile or so into the town with Newman's body slung over his saddle.

To say that the sheriff had been surprised would be the understatement of the year. He had listened to Roland's explanation eagerly.

'At least it will save us the cost of a trial,' he had exclaimed. 'You'll stay the night, of course,' he added.

'I've already made up Roland's bed,' announced his wife.

So Roland had spent a delightful evening with his friends. He had eaten an enjoyable meal – a chicken pie with plenty of vegetables and potatoes.

'You still need some good food inside you,'

Emma had commented. While they were enjoying a glass of wine she said, 'Have you asked May to marry you, yet?'

'Emma,' protested her startled husband. 'You can't ask our guest a question like that.'

'If I can't ask him, who can?' she demanded.

'It's all right,' said Roland, hastily. 'I can answer the question.'

'Well?' demanded Emma, with eager anticipation.

'I'm afraid I haven't asked her yet,' admitted Roland.

'Well my advice is to ask her sooner rather than later. She's head over heels in love with you.'

The sheriff, seeing Roland's embarrassment had tactfully changed the subject. Now the other awkward question kept re-occurring as Roland rode along. Was he in love with May?

He certainly liked her a lot. In fact there was no other woman he would prefer to be with. He could easily imagine himself spending the rest of his life with her. There was no other woman in his life to stop him doing just that. True there had been a brief affair when he was in Boston, but that had come to a sudden end. Now there was no woman on the horizon. Except Hedda, a small voice prompted.

Hedda. She was the most beautiful woman he had ever met. That included some of the attractive young ladies he had known in Boston. In the first place Hedda had regarded him as the lowest of the low, blaming him for her brother's death. But the two of them had certainly seemed to be on friendly terms when he had left the Olsen ranch the last time.

Well there was some unfinished business to attend to before he contemplated his future. When he finally arrived at May's cottage the obvious delight on her face at seeing him return safely almost made him change his mind. He was on the point of kissing her expectant face when he banished the thought.

'I've got some good news for you,' he said.

She tried unsuccessfully to hide her disappointment that he hadn't kissed her.

'You'd better come in,' she said.

When they were in the living-room Roland began, 'In the first place Newman is dead. I was forced to kill him when he tried to shoot me with a small hand-pistol which he had hidden in his jacket. I took his body into Crichton. The sheriff is clearing up the affair.'

'I'm glad he's dead,' said May, simply.

'So that's over,' continued Roland. 'There's one other thing. This.' He produced the document which she had signed transferring the Olsen farm solely to Newman. 'He won't be needing this where he's going. So it's not a legal document any longer. Anyhow it was never properly witnessed, although no doubt Newman would have found a couple of villains in a saloon to witness it. So, since it's no use to anyone there's only one thing to do with it.'

'What's that?' asked a puzzled May.

'I'll show you.' Roland went through into the kitchen. May followed him. She watched while Roland held the document over the fire. He dropped it into the fire where it burned slowly for a moment then curled up and slowly disintegrated as the flames licked it.

While May made some coffee Roland sprang one more surprise on her. 'That means that you now own the Olsen ranch,' he announced.

'Yes, I suppose it does,' said May, thoughtfully. 'Since everything Richard owned came to me. Now Newman is dead, then, all the Olsens' land is mine.'

'One thousand acres,' Roland reminded her, as he accepted the coffee.

'I don't want the land,' she said, with surprising venom. 'I don't want to be a part of a crooked deal. Anyhow I think there's something unlucky about the land. Your brother was killed going across it. You were almost killed because of it. I've been almost raped because of it. I don't want anything to do with it.'

'There is one way out. You could give it back to Olsen for the original hundred dollars he paid for it. That way the slate would be wiped clean.'

'Yes, it would, wouldn't it,' said May, thoughtfully.

'I could ride out to the Olsen ranch and tell them.'

May hesitated. She had seen the beautiful Hedda at her brother's funeral. She had also seen the look of hatred with which she had regarded Roland. It was obvious that they would be enemies for life. So why was she hesitating? Perhaps it was because Roland hadn't kissed her when she had all but offered her lips to him about half an hour ago. Maybe there was a slight fear that he cared for another woman. A woman who could be Hedda.

She dismissed the thought. It seemed too preposterous. After all he had only seen her twice as far as she knew.

'Right. Go ahead and tell him. Say that I'll see that the necessary document is drawn up. This time it will be legal.' She managed a smile.

Roland rode happily out to the Olsen ranch. Soon he would be able to explain to Olsen that his ranch would really be his. He would own it to do whatever he wished with it. If he wished to sell part of it to the railway company then that would be his choice. At least all the dealing would be legal and above board. He wouldn't just be waiting for the shares to rocket up before making a killing on the stock market, as Newman had planned.

As he swung his horse into the lane which would lead to the Olsen ranch, he was aware of the sound of gunfire. He was seized with a dreadful premonition as he spurred his horse into a gallop.

His worst fears were justified; there was a gunfight in progress between Moss Lampton's cowboys and the Olsens. He rode though the cornfield ignoring the persistent bullets. He knew that one stray shot could end his life, as it had ended John's when he came this way several weeks before.

He reached the wall behind which the Olsens were hiding in safety. His horse jumped the wall and he drew up in the compound.

'That wasn't a very clever thing to do,' said Mr Olsen, hardly looking up from the rifle he was holding.

'It was brave though,' said another voice. It was Hedda. She, too, was holding a rifle.

Roland felt exhilarated at her words. He felt he would have run the gauntlet of coming though the cornfield again, just to hear them.

'Are you with us, Deputy?' It was Nils.

Well he certainly wasn't with Childs. He accepted the rifle that Nils handed him.

'How long has this been going on?' he demanded.

'About half an hour,' Nils replied. 'They've wounded one of our cousins. Not seriously, I think. And we've wounded one of their men.'

At least nobody had been killed yet, that was something to be thankful for, concluded Roland.

The thought had barely surfaced when Hedda, who was crouched beside him suddenly gave a groan and toppled backwards. Roland assumed that she had been grazed by a stray bullet. Yes, there was the blood in her blonde hair to prove it. Suddenly a terrible fear gripped him. Had she merely been grazed, or worse? He stared at her sightless eyes and immediately knew the answer.

He was seized by a wild madness. Without heeding the bullets he suddenly stood up.

'Stop shooting,' he cried.

Whether it was the unexpected sight of him standing up in the face of the bullets which were peppering the compound, or the fact that many of Moss Lampton's cowboys recognized him he would never know, but suddenly the firing ceased.

'You've just killed the most beautiful woman I've ever met.' His voice was choked with emotion. 'One of your bullets killed her. Why?' His voice cracked as he roared the question.

'Because we want Olsen off this land.' The voice that answered was Childs's.

'He's got more right to this land than you've got to yours,' shouted Roland. 'He's got the law on his side.'

'We've got the guns on ours,' sneered Childs.

Roland took a deep breath. 'In that case we'll

let the guns settle it. It's you and me Childs. If I win your men will all go back to the ranch.'

Childs stepped fully into view. There was an arrogance in his stance which said: the last time you backed down from a gunfight. What makes you think you've got a chance now?

Roland vaulted over the wall and began to walk slowly towards Childs. He had never hated a man so much in his life. Childs was directly responsible for starting the gunfight. Therefore he was responsible for killing his beautiful Hedda.

Childs had taken up his stance in the middle of the corn. He watched Roland's slow progress towards him. He had already killed six men and he knew with unwavering certainty that he would make the lawman his seventh. He licked his lips in pleasurable anticipation as he watched Roland's slow approach.

The Olsens had stood up from the safety of the cover of the wall and were watching Roland. Even Mr Olsen had stopped in the act of carrying Hedda's body into the ranch and was following Roland's progress.

Childs was calculating when to go for his gun. All his previous fights had been in saloons where he and his opponent had been facing each other. This gunfight presented a slightly different problem since Roland was coming towards him. Childs knew that if he drew too soon and Roland was too far away then there was a slight possibility that he would miss. The other flicker of doubt that crossed his mind was that he was looking into the sun. He hadn't realized it before but the sun was only just above the horizon. This meant that he was looking directly into it. Not only that but he had already been looking into it for several minutes as Roland made his slow way towards him. He blinked rapidly to clear his eyes of any blurred image they were retaining.

'What's the matter, Childs, afraid to go for your gun?' taunted Roland.

Suddenly Childs realized that everything had changed. Whereas a few minutes ago he had been completely in charge, now Roland was the one who was confident, even taunting him.

Damn him! He would show him.

Childs went for his gun. Roland drew at the same time. Whether it was the seeds of doubt which had been planted in Childs's mind or the fact that looking into the sun had blurred his vision would never be known. What was soon apparent, however, was that Childs had missed with his shot. He didn't have a chance to try a second. Roland's bullet hit him in the heart. For good measure Roland put several more bullets into him.

The following day the story about Roland's success in the gunfight reached May. She hurried to Mrs Pine's house. When she saw Mrs Pine's face she knew that something was amiss.

'Roland wasn't injured was he?' she gasped.

'No, but he's gone,' announced a distraught Mrs Pine.

'Gone? What do you mean, gone?'

'He caught the morning stage out of town. He left your horse tied up in the back. He said he was going back to Boston.'

'I see,' said May. Although in truth she didn't see anything clearly. Why had he suddenly gone back to Boston after the scene of his triumph in killing the arch-villain Childs? Why hadn't he come to say goodbye to her?

She returned to her cottage. It suddenly seemed more empty than ever. Although Roland had only come into the cottage on a few occasions, it was the fact that she knew he was living only a short distance away which had somehow seemed to fill it with his presence.

In fact he didn't come to the cottage for the next three months. When he did eventually present himself at the door, it was with abject apology written all over his face.

'The prodigal has returned,' he stated.

'You'd better come in,' said May, coldly.

'There is one thing,' said Roland, as he made no move to enter the house.

'What's that?' demanded a puzzled May.

'Do you remember when you were nursing me back to health in Crichton. You said that you had a dream that you would like to ride like the wind on a fast horse. You would then find a secluded spot to stop. And then make love.'

May regarded him steadily. Suddenly all the doubts and frustration which he had caused her during the past months seemed to melt away. Suddenly her face split into a smile. It was the loveliest expression that Roland had seen for ages. He knew he would cherish it for the rest of his life.

'Well?' she demanded.

'I've got a fast horse waiting outside,' he announced.

'Wait here until I get mine,' she said.